Grande Jete'

a novel

Amy Shomshak

To Fiona
a Beautiful
Ballerina!
Love,
Amy

Albert's Bridge Books

Published by Albert's Bridge Books
Minneapolis, MN
Although real places and institutions are depicted in this book, they are used in the service of fiction. No character in this book is based on any person, living or dead, and the world presented is completely fictitious.

Manufactured in the United Sates of America

Library of Congress Cataloging-in-Publication Data
Gaspard, Amy, 1961-
Slender Thread, A (Grande Jete') / Amy Shomshak

Copyright TXu001816582

Cover Design
John Gaspard/miljko

For my wonderful husband, John,
my sister, Margaret Berkowitz, my niece, Sarah
Berkowitz, my mother Helen Louise Shomshak,
who died of cancer in 2012, and for all the girls
who have come to me for ballet lessons over the
past twenty years.

Thanks to my ballet instructors: Lirena Branitski, formerly of the Bolshoi and Kiev Opera Ballets, Eugene Collins of Ballet Russe de Monte Carlo, Loyce Houlton of Minnesota Dance Theater, Lyudmila Kudrashova of the Kirov Ballet Academy, Bonnie Mathis of American Ballet Theater, Maya Plissetskaya of the Bolshoi Ballet, and Marjorie Thompson of New York City Ballet. Thanks to Melissa Grannis and the Dance Connection for giving me a loving place to teach ballet and to choreograph. Thanks to all who made it possible for me to train and study in Russia time and time again.

"Unexpected travels ... are dancing lessons from God"

Kurt Vonnegut

Chapter One

Her uncle's house felt cold to Gina, and damp. She rounded the corner on the walk home from school and shivered looking at it. Uncle Eugene's white and grey house was three stories tall with gardens surrounded by a curling black iron fence. It was two hour's drive from her old house in Minneapolis. Her uncle's house in Northfield might as well have been on another planet. Gina sighed and took the mail out of the box. She unlocked the heavy door with her key.

She looked at herself for a moment in the mirror on the closet door as she hung up her coat. Gina was twelve and a half. She was dark-haired, small, and slender like her mother had been. Born to dance, she had heard people say.

Gina shut the closet door. She didn't take off her navy uniform sweater. It was late February of 1991. Although it was growing warmer everyday, it was winter in Minnesota. The afternoon had a dark early evening feeling. She hugged her arms to herself.

Her gaze shifted to the open curving staircase and she watched for her cat, Nijinsky, to come out. Gina walked on polished wooden floors through large beautiful rooms with graceful furniture to the kitchen. Everything was neatly arranged according to her Uncle Gene's wishes. No soft mounds of clothes were strewn about. There was not a single strain of music to stir up painful memories of her mother.

Nijinsky appeared and brushed his grey-striped face against her ankles. She missed Nijinsky all day at school.

Having hugged Nijinsky, Gina put him down to sit by her ankles. Out of deep green eyes she looked at the mail. There was nothing from her father. There never was.

He had left Gina and her mother when Gina was eight. She remembered hearing her mother arguing with him when he was drunk. Even so, Gina looked for him at her mother's funeral. He never appeared.

A week after her mother's funeral Gina came to Northfield to live with her Uncle Eugene. Gina left her old school, her old home, and ballet lessons behind. She was miserably forced to attend St. Elizabeth's Middle School near her uncle's house.

She looked at the notice of parent-teacher conferences from St. Elizabeth's that was in the mail. Today at school hadn't been quite so awful, she thought. Considering it was only slightly less awful than the day before.

Gina thought of the girls at school this morning. A smug girl, surrounded by a pack of her horrid friends, had come up to Gina at her locker.

The snobby girl asked, "Is it true that your mother died of cancer?"

"What? What do you know about my mother?" asked Gina in surprise.

"Oh, Mrs. Murdock told us to be nice to you because your mother died." The girls stood around and waited for Gina to answer.

\"Mrs. Murdock! She said that to you!?" Gina stepped back in shock.

"What kind of cancer was it, anyway? Are you afraid you'll get cancer someday?" one of the other girls pressed.

"That's none of your business!" Gina shot back.

"I only ask because if there are other students like you here, maybe I could get up a little grief club. I'm president of the eighth grade. It's my duty to see that our student body is well-served."

"Leave me alone!" Gina almost shouted.

Gina wanted to punch her. It would have hurt, too, with those braces on her teeth. Gina chose instead to loudly slam her locker door. She gave her long, dark hair a toss and walked away. She heard the voices of the girls behind her, "Can you believe that? I was just trying to be nice."

Gina set the mail down on her uncle's kitchen counter with a similar slam. She hugged Nijinsky again. She fed him his dinner. He liked only dry, crunchy cat food, day in and day out. Yesterday her Uncle Gene brought home liver, shrimp, and lobster-flavored treats to entice Nijinsky. Gina knew from the excitement in his voice when he called for Nijinsky, that he had a new brand of kitty treat. Then she heard his sigh as Nijinsky gave one sniff and turned away in revulsion

Her uncle, Dr. Eugene Shostek, was a professor in the Russian Studies department at Carlton College. He was tall, dark-haired, and starting to grey. At forty-five years old, he was handsome and youthful. Dr. Shostek, was known as "Gene" to family and friends. He had sparkling charm and a kind heart.

Gene had visited Russia many times to work or to study. Russia is often called "The Land of Ballet" and Gene had gone many times to see beautiful ballet performances when he was there. His sister, Lily, was Gina's mom. Lily asked Gene to take of Gina when she knew she was dying.

In the kitchen at Gene's house the phone rang. Gina picked it up, hearing Uncle Gene's voice.

"Yes, Uncle Gene, I got in just fine. I answered the phone didn't I?"

"Yes, Nijinsky is fine, too."

"No, the stove is not on."

"Uncle Gene, you ask me the same stuff every day!"

"Yes, I'll do my homework. I love you, too. Bye." Gina replaced the receiver. Gina knew her uncle worked late because he loved being a professor of Russian. So much that he wanted her to learn the Russian language, too!

Last Sunday evening, Gene sat Gina down in the dining room to teach her the Russian alphabet. Gina could hear the seconds ticking away from the grandfather clock in the hall. Gina found Russian monstrously confusing. She gazed politely at the books Gene placed in front of her. All the while she planned her escape. She finally burst out, "Uncle Gene, I don't need to know the Russian alphabet!"

"But it would be excellent for you to know it!" Patiently she listened to his *Learn the Russian Alphabet* lecture that he gave to university students. "Two little old monks, Cyril and Methodius sat down one day and wrote the Russian alphabet. Isn't that fascinating?"

"Fascinating? Are you kidding?" Gina looked at him in disbelief.

"It's not as foreign as you think. Look at these letters, Gina, you already know them."

She looked over the letters, "A, Z, K, M, O, T." He crowed, "There you've already knocked off six of them!"

"Uncle Gene, there are twenty eight more letters. The Russian C is an S, P is an R, and H is an N. That's not even counting the letters that don't even look like letters!" she pleaded. She pointed to the alphabet in front of her. "See that! That's a squiggle!"

"Gina, my dear, some day I know you will thank me for teaching you the Russian language. We might travel on the Trans-Siberian railway together in winter! And you will become a Russian ballerina! How delightful!"

"Uncle Gene, I will not eat borscht and wear woolen scarves on my head! No way! And no more ballet!" Gina shuddered at the thought.

He ignored her and went on. "Learn this letter with a picture. For example, look at the letter X. It makes a harsh 'H' sound, right? So if you imagine a pair of HOCKEY sticks crossed in an X, you'll remember the sound 'H!'" He had removed his suit coat and tie at this point.

"But, Uncle Gene, what if I remember HUBCAP instead of HOCKEY sticks and end up with an O instead of an X?" She begged off to go to her room. Gene sadly put the books away as Gina disappeared down the hall.

She sat down on her new bed in her uncle's house. Gina had loved her mother's funny old house in Minneapolis. It had been built in the year 1910 and was forever falling apart. The doors and staircases creaked, doorknobs fell off in their hands, and the faucets leaked. Gina and her mother were sure the place was haunted. Gina had loved all of its nooks and crannies and messes and joy.

Mostly she missed her mother, Lily. Her mother was a ballet teacher. She taught Gina her very first steps. Gina got up from her bed. She looked into the mirror above the dresser. She made slow graceful, movements with her arms.

When Gina was four years old she began dancing in the mirror after she saw ballet dancers on television. By the time she was eight years old she loved to listen to Debussy's *L' Apres Midi d' Un Faun*. It was so beautiful it made her cry. Gina knew there was something delicate and graceful about herself.

She picked up her pink satin pointe shoes from the dresser and held them. In Minneapolis Gina had loved pointe shoes, ballet lessons, and her last teacher, Madame Branitskaya, who was from Russia. Gina lay back on the bed, staring at the ceiling, picturing her mother in her mind. She remembered Lily's voice from one of the last times she was with her in the hospital.

"Gina, did you practice your dancing?" Lily had asked sitting up in bed.

"Of course, I did mom. Watch this!" Gina had learned a new step. She executed a springy "pas de basque" perfectly for her mom.

"Gina, that is wonderful!" she remembered Lily exclaiming in delight.

Gina slowly put her pointe shoes back into their pink, mesh bag and set them back on the dresser. For two long months, since moving in with her uncle, she hadn't danced at all. She didn't have the heart to practice. Gina felt too sad. Her heart was empty and she hurt. She would never hear Lily's voice again.

She sat down on the floor. She hated crying, but she couldn't seem to stop herself. She tried to cry quietly so that her Uncle Gene wouldn't hear her. She hated it even more when he came in and tried to comfort her. She heard a soft knock at the door.

"Uncle Gene, I'm okay," she sniffled, getting tissues from the dresser.

"Would you like to like to watch the news with me?" he gently asked.

"I'm really okay. I'm going to bed." She blew her nose.

"All right, dear Gina. Sweet dreams."

"You, too, Uncle Gene."

She put on her nightgown and climbed into bed. Gina burrowed her head into her pillow. She remembered her first recital for Madame Branitskaya. She had been sick to her stomach and ran away from the theater.

"I don't have enough courage to dance in the theater, anyway. It's a good thing I quit," she said to herself. Gina found herself talking to the ceiling, "Mom, you used to promise me you would teach me how to get over stage fright. Now you're gone and it's too late! Anyway, no one cares if I dance or not. Even if I did, they wouldn't like it."

Gina turned her radio on to the classical station with the volume on very low. Even if Uncle Gene heard the radio, she knew he wouldn't mind her listening to classical music. A piece of music was playing that her mother had danced to, the music by Tchaikovsky for *The Russian Dance* in the *Nutcracker Fantasy* ballet.

Gina thought that she would never be able to perform on stage the beautiful way her mother had. Gina loved to watch her mother do the simplest things, like walking. There was something so breathlessly delicate and powerful about Lily's walk.

"I miss you, mom." Gina turned over and tried to go to sleep.

Chapter Two

Gina woke up. It was still night. In the moonlight she could see the picture of her mother on her nightstand. She looked at her mother smiling back at her. She remembered the afternoon in June when Lily told Gina she was sick. Lily had called Gina onto the sunny porch. They sat down in the swing together.

"Gina," she began.

"Yes, mama."

As gently as a mother could tell her daughter, she told Gina that a cancer had grown inside of her. She told Gina that it was too late for any doctors or any cure to do anything to save her. She would have to leave Gina soon. And Gina would have to go to live with her Uncle Gene.

"I need you to promise me some things, as hard as you have ever promised to do anything. I need you to promise with your whole self and heart and soul that you will do them." Lily put her arm around Gina.

"Yes, mama." Gina snuggled closer.

"Take care of your uncle for me. Mess up his house every now and then. Hang the paintings in his study so they're all a bit off kilter. Serve him pizza for breakfast sometimes. Make sure he watches cartoons with you and takes you on the roller coaster at the State Fair every summer.

"Mama," Gina sniffled. "Uncle Gene hates the roller coaster."

"Exactly. Make him go anyway and tell him I said so. And when the time comes don't be interested too much in boys. Always remember how beautiful and lovely you are. Someday when you are older a man who is meant only for you will come and love you as much as I do. You will begin a life with him and help each other to be happy." Lily dabbed her eyes.

"Yes, mama."

"And Gina, know that you are talented. You have a special gift in your dancing. Know that you are precious, and worth all of the diamonds and gold and rubies and emeralds in the world."

"Yes, mama." Both were crying and rocking and hugging.

"And know that wherever you are, I love you. That your uncle loves you and that even though I have to die, I will never, ever leave you, not even for a second. Most of all, Gina, know that you love you, and all of the wonderful things about yourself."

Gina and Lily sat on that swing for a long time that afternoon. The sun slipped away covering them in shade. Lily died the following November in the middle of a snowstorm. Gina turned over in her bed and stared at the ceiling. Gina still wished she could have gone with her mother.

Lily slowly awakened and thought about Gina. Lily had been in the attic of her house in Minneapolis for quite some time. She sat on a slender chair. Her cheek rested on her hand. Her elbow rested on the edge of a fragile writing desk. Lily felt quite light and comfortable.

She thought, "I feel a little too light." She looked through her hand to the desk below. She looked down at her cream-colored gown whose hem lapped around her ankles above bare feet. She looked right through herself to the floor. "I am a ghost! How very delightful! And such wonderful costuming!"

The ghostly Lily looked around the room. A tutu and its bodice were the centerpiece of the round room with its opaque, curved windows. All was white and covered with glistening frost. Lily sat through day and night and over again. The sun traveled across the windows. Slowly light shone around the room to remind her that time was passing.

A deep, enveloping joy was in her. At times tears rolled down her face and neck. She sat motionless. She missed Gina so terribly. A speck of frost on a shiny piece of costume glistened in her eye. "I've been so silly! I'm a ghost! I can see Gina anytime I want, even if she can't see me! Off to Uncle Gene's house!" she said as she flew out of the room.

Chapter Three

The following afternoon Gina was at her locker. She heard voices near her. "It better not be those awful girls again," she muttered under her breath. The girls came closer.

Gina heard the president of the eighth grade say to her friends, "Did you know the English teacher, Miss McReynolds, has a crush on Gina's uncle?"

"What?! How does she know him? Isn't she engaged to the gym teacher, Mr. Halvorson?!" the girls squealed.

"The uncle showed up at conferences for Gina, because she doesn't have any real parents. McReynolds saw him and fell for him," the girl said, pretending to faint in a romantic swoon. "It gets better. Halvorson said something rude to the uncle, and..." She paused as the girls gathered around her. "Then, the uncle punched Halvorson! He's got a huge black eye!" All of the girls laughed as they continued past Gina down the hallway.

Gina slammed her locker shut, left St. Elizabeth's, breaking a million rules, and marched home. She knew her uncle would be there. He did not give lectures at the university on Thursdays. She flung open the door of the den. Gene was at his desk. His face was covered by the *Journal of the American Council of Teachers of Russian.* She snatched it out of his hands.

"Uncle Gene, you have gone crazy! People just don't go around hitting each other!" she fairly shouted.

"Gina, what is the matter?" Gene asked, calmly taking the magazine out of her trembling hands.

"You punched my gym teacher in the face!" Gina accused. "At parent-teacher conferences yesterday, you hit him in the face! And you didn't tell me!"

"I most certainly did not. I would not waste my strength on a dolt like Halvorson. The man insists that people call him 'Skip,' for heaven's sake. If I ever again have to listen to how he kicked the winning pass at his college football game, I will pop him," tensely explained Gene.

"Uncle Gene, you don't kick a pass. You throw one, or catch one. But that doesn't matter. I can't go to school tomorrow! Everyone is saying that the English teacher, Miss McReynolds, is in love with you. She's engaged to Halvorson! And all the kids are saying that you let him have it! He has a huge black eye! How could you?" Gina angrily said. She stomped around the office.

"Gina, listen to me. At school yesterday, that oaf Halvorson was tearing around a corner. He bumped into me in the hall. He knocked the book I was carrying to the floor. Skipper Boy bent down to pick it up for me. As he arose his face came in contact with my elbow, the result of which was a black eye. It is not my fault that Miss McReynolds is unhappy with her choice of fiancé. If Skippy ever cracked a book himself, she might find him more interesting."

"No one's going to believe that! I can't ever go to school again! I won't!" Gina said as she stood and stamped her foot.

Gene stood up from his desk chair. "I expect you to ignore any rumors that have come about because of this. You will attend school, as well as gym class, as usual."

"I can't! It's too awful!" Gina pleaded.

"You will. You can expect my checking daily to see that you do!" insisted Gene. Both walked in silence back to St. Elizabeth's. Gene walked with her to the office to check her in, and he walked her to her classroom and watched her take her seat.

The following Friday morning Gina was sipping her cocoa. Her uncle came into the dining room and sat down. She prayed he wasn't going to bring up how she broke rules by leaving school again. "Morning, Uncle Gene. Aren't you going to the university today?"

"As a matter of fact I am not. How did you know?" He smiled at her and set down a cup of tea.

"You're not wearing your teaching armor," Gina said wiping whipped cream off of her upper lip with a napkin.

"My teaching what?" Gene looked confused.

"You know, your teaching armor, that tweed coat and wool tie and pants you wear to the university. I don't know how you stand it. They're so scratchy I can't be by you without sneezing or rubbing my eyes."

Gene smiled again. "Gina, I am not going in to teach today. We have matters that need to be taken care of. You are not attending school today, either."

She mentally sent a sneer of triumph to the snobby eight-grade president and her creepy friends. "In fact," he continued, "I have something important to report. We are going to move. I have accepted a position at the consulate in Leningrad. We are moving to Russia, at least for a year."

Gina stood up numbly, unable to speak. "What! Russia?! No! Are you crazy? I don't want to...I feel sick! I mean I hate school and everything, but move again! You're crazy!"

"Gina, please sit down. I am not crazy. I know you do not like the school here. Spending a year in another country might be good for you right now. I admit, I have been waiting all of my life for a chance like this, to work at the consulate in Leningrad. If you don't want to go with me, you could stay with Aunt Maggie and Uncle Robert. You could go to school in Minneapolis with their children."

Gina thought about that. "My cousins are nice, but all they care about is playing stupid sports. Mom always wanted to go to Russia. Oh, Uncle Gene, I don't know! Wait a minute, what's a consulate?" she finally managed to ask.

"The American consulate in Leningrad is the residence for officials from the United States who represent the interests of American citizens in the U.S.S.R.," answered Gene.

"What the heck? I never know what you're talking about!" Gina said waving her hands in the air. She scowled at her uncle as Gene said, "I'll explain more later, let's go!"

"Where?" she asked as she grabbed a jacket and followed him out the door.

Feeling queasy and in shock, Gina went with her uncle that day to have a physical. They filled prescriptions for antibiotics in case they needed them in Russia. Waiting in line at the drugstore, she asked Gene, "Why can't we just go to a doctor in Russia if we need antibiotics?"

"Prescription drugs are hard to come by there. There are not enough antibiotics for everyone who needs them. I imagine they have medicine at the consulate, but who knows?" Gene answered, accepting the white prescription bag from the pharmacist. Next they went to Kinko's where Gina had her picture taken for her passport. From there they went to St. Elizabeth's to unenroll her from school. Gina liked that part the best. Lastly, they went to their favorite Italian restaurant.

As they sat down at their table Gina looked at her uncle and said, "Uncle Gene, I haven't felt normal since before mom was sick. Mom dying and moving here is like a bad dream. Or a nightmare. I know you're trying to help me, but now this?"

Gene twisted his napkin. "I hope I am not being selfish in asking you to go with me, Gina. Somehow I know it is what Lily would have wanted for you."

Gina looked down at the table. "I know mom would want me to go, too. But I don't think Russia will be any better. Everything is grey and rainy without mom. Russia isn't going to cure that. Uncle Gene, what about Nijinsky?" Gina was almost afraid to ask.

"I think he will be happiest going to live with your Aunt Maggie. I know how much you will miss him. Maggie will take good care of him. I think I can arrange for you to adopt a kitten while we are in Russia. You will have to leave the kitten when you come home. But you will know that you will be returning to Nijinsky," Gene suggested.

Gina relaxed slightly, knowing that Nijinsky would be safe with Aunt Maggie. Lily and her sister Maggie had been very close. Gina often wished that she had someone other than Nijinsky with whom to share her troubles and fun. She didn't have one special friend to whom she might tell everything. Gina admitted to Gene, "This restaurant is one nice thing about living with you."

"I am happy you enjoy this place, Gina. It is a restaurant that has been credited by Italy as serving only authentic Tuscan dishes."

"Whatever. I like the spaghetti. I bet mom would like it, too." Gina imagined how Lily would like it and became sad. "Uncle Gene

I am afraid of forgetting mom, but I feel so awful when I do remember. Why can't she still be here?"

"I do not know, Gina. I miss my sister very much. I am glad that you are here with me."

Gina twirled her spaghetti. "I love the idea of leaving St. Elizabeth's. I hate thinking of being without Nijinsky for a whole year. The trip would be awful for him. Strange Russian cats that carry strange Russian diseases might infect him." She shuddered. "It would be terrifying for him in the baggage compartment on the airplane. Once I read in the newspaper about this woman who flew her cat somewhere. The baggage people let him out of his cage. He was lost forever."

Gene looked up from his risotto. "Gina, I am certain that we cannot take Nijinsky with us. The consulate will not allow it."

"Well, I guess it will be all right if Nijinsky stays with Aunt Maggie and Uncle Robert. But that Russian kitten will have to be pretty nice or no deal. And no giving it some dumb Russian name that no one except you can say," Gina insisted.

"Something purely American for a name, I suppose like, say, oh...let me think... Nijinsky, perhaps?" Gene said as he looked over the tops of his glasses at his niece.

"Oh, Uncle Gene, stop it! I know my cat is named after a Russian dancer. But I picked it myself," Gina smiled back at him. "So, where are we going anyway? You talk about Russia and the U.S.S.R. and the Soviet Union. You talk about Leningrad and St. Petersburg. I don't get it. Are they all the same place?"

"Russia is part of the U.S.S.R., which is the Union of Soviet Socialist Republics. It is also called the Soviet Union. Leningrad is a city in Russia that used to be called St. Petersburg," Gene explained.

"You're kidding, right? That made no sense. Is everything there confusing? Do they really need to keep changing the names of stuff? Gina asked, feeling anxious and annoyed.

Their server came by and Gene ordered tiramisu for them to share. "I will explain everything as well as I can. We are going to live in an apartment on Rubinstein Street, just off of Nevsky Avenue in Leningrad. The name of the city may change again to St. Petersburg."

"Again, you make no sense! That's it. I'm not going. This is ridiculous! I can't even say where I'm going to live!" Gina lowered her voice as their dessert arrived.

"I will help you. I promise. The entire form of government is changing in Russia. It is complicated," he remarked.

"When are we leaving? You had to do some pretty fast talking to get Old Lady Murdock to enter my last test score as end of the year final grades. Besides, it's only March. Does this mean I'm done with school for the year?" Gina asked. She thought that there might be a silver lining after all.

"You most certainly have not completed your academic requirements for the year. I signed off on your report card to save Mrs. Murdock sending it to me in Russia. Postal service to and from Russia is so slow that we might never receive it at all. I simply signed off on it now, with the understanding that I will see to it that you complete all of the course work for the eighth grade by the middle of June. There is nothing more appropriate. I am, after all, a teacher," said Gene.

"Uncle Gene, you're a university professor who's slumming! You're the worst!" Gina exclaimed.

"Gina, there is nothing wrong with the way that I instruct. I am deeply hurt by your suggesting that I am less than adequate as a teacher," said Gene. He didn't have a trace of understanding of his niece's plight.

"It's not that. You're a great teacher, just not for me. You explain every little thing so much I can't understand it! Now I'm never going to get out of eighth grade!" Gina cried.

"There is no need for hysterics," Gene sighed. "Your mother and Maggie said the same thing about me. I shall look into sending you to the International School in Leningrad. I wanted you to have a purely Russian experience. However, it may be best for you to attend the International School there."

Gina spooned up the last bit of her tiramisu. "What's the International School?"

"The International School is for children of diplomats who work in Leningrad. The education is exceptional. Naturally, courses are available in the Russian language taught by native speakers," explained Gene.

"Thrilling," thought Gina resisting the temptation to roll her eyes. She answered instead, "All right, I'll give it a try. Don't they have any classes with teachers who speak English?"

"Gina, I promise I will check. I suspect you shall want to resume ballet lessons in Leningrad. The instruction is the best in the world."

"No, Uncle Gene. I don't do ballet anymore. It was just a stupid kid thing I used to do," Gina firmly replied.

"Well, that remains to be seen. We shall ask for our check and go home. I am exhausted," Gene said as he motioned for the waiter.

"It's not exactly home anymore, is it?" remarked Gina as she put on her sweater.

As she was changing into her nightgown, Gina heard a muffled bump come from the ceiling above her. "Must be a squirrel on the roof or in the attic," she thought.

Lily rubbed the spot on her head where she had bumped the ceiling. Lily was floating in the corner of Gina's room. "I just don't have the walking thing down, yet. It's more fun to fly anyway!" She flew around the room. She stopped to hover over Gina's bed. Lily gently hugged her arms around her soft self and her silky dress. Lily gave off a little glow. The room was sparkling and held her like a diamond in the night sky. She traced Gina's name in the glittering air that surrounded her.

"Oh, Gina," Lily thought. "I love you so much!"

Chapter Four

The following Saturday Gina woke up smiling. "Ahhh, no more pruney Old Lady Murdock. No more simpy class presidents. No more punched-in-the-face gym teachers. No more fiancées who have crushes on my own uncle," thought Gina. She snuggled closer to Nijinsky. She had not gone to school for a whole week. It felt wonderful. Gina had studied at home. She prepared the last of her homework to be submitted to St. Elizabeth's before they left for Leningrad.

"Gina, get up, please. We have a long day ahead of us," Gene called up the stairs to his niece. "Gina!"

"All right, all right already," mumbled Gina. She put on clothes and stumbled down the stairs to the dining room. "It's Saturday. Why are we up so early?"

"Today, my dear, we are going to transform you into a proper visitor to Russia." Seeing the look on Gina's face he said, "No, no, not the alphabet again. We are going shopping. We are leaving for Leningrad in a week. You cannot go wearing the clothes that you have."

"I will not wear a woolen scarf on my head. I don't care how cold it gets. They itch! And no blouses with embroidery on the front that some old lady made. And absolutely no big, fluffy white bows in my hair! I swear, I won't leave the house, not ever, not for a whole year!" Gina stood up. Her voice rose to a crescendo of anger and fear at the thought of having to dress like some stupid Anastasia.

"Gina, calm down. I only suggest that you wear dresses to school and on Sundays. Avoid bright, garish colors, and no shorts or any of those little t-shirt things you wear in the summer. We shall discuss the woolen scarf issue when winter comes. I do not want you taking ill your first winter in Leningrad."

"First winter," Gina thought. That meant he was considering more than one. He switched out things around the house with Russian ones. In the last few days he had started her drinking tea with sugar out of little glasses sitting in metal holders. They were hot as the dickens if you tried to pick them up. "Stakani and podstakani'" he said they were called. No more cocoa. And no more raspberry granola bars for breakfast. Now they had "kasha," he called it. Which wasn't too bad, she gratefully discovered, as long as it was drowned in honey and milk. And "taking ill" for heaven's sake. He's been reading those Russian novels again. She knew it.

Her uncle loved to read endless Russian novels in which nothing ever happened. Gina knew. All of the characters sat around drinking tea, having headaches, and waiting for something to happen. Nothing ever did. Finally someone died. Then everyone talked about the emptiness of life. Or something like that.

Gina had heard her uncle and his friends from the University discussing those silly Russian books. Now Gina watched him glide around the house in his best suits. He started smoking a pipe and gazed out onto the lawn a lot. He stopped acting like Uncle Gene and started acting like *Uncle Vanya.*

And now the wardrobe changes. Gina knew if her uncle had his way she would be decked out in a huge hat with flowers on it. She would have to wear lace gloves. Worse yet, he would make her carry a parasol. She imagined scenes in her life flash by in Leningrad. He would make her sit in straight-backed chairs memorizing poetry. Then, horror of all horrors, he would force her to recite verses to his Russian friends.

Gina snapped back to the present. "Don't you think maybe we should wait until we get there before we start living out *Doctor Zhivago?* I'll go shopping with you, but I like my own clothes."

At the end of the day they returned with four skirts for fall and winter and three long dresses for summer and spring. They found cotton sweaters in various soft colors, and black walking shoes that Gina liked. They bought a new silk tie for Gene. Gina insisted that he buy it. Its rich, deep grey color pointed out his eyes and the light parts of his salt and pepper hair. Gina knew Lily would have liked to see him wear it.

That Sunday Aunt Maggie came to pick up Nijinsky. Gina missed him so much she was glad to be leaving. There was no reason to spend one more minute in Minnesota without Nijinsky.

Their last day was strange. Gina found herself standing uncertainly in the garage. She watched her uncle pack up the last of the boxes. He methodically placed them in a pile marked, "Leningrad." She wondered if somewhere in heaven her mother knew that Gina was going to miss eighth grade graduation.

A few weeks ago at school Gina read the announcements about graduation. It would be held in the garden in the back of the school on an evening in June. There would be awards. The seventh graders would serve a farewell dinner. Gina overheard the other girls talking about what kind of dresses they would have. The eighth graders had already started autographing ribbons. Each graduate was given two long wide ribbons in the school colors on which friends signed their names. Gina knew she would not be at the ceremony. She threw hers away.

"Uncle Gene, I'm going to miss my graduation from St. Elizabeth's," Gina said.

"What difference does it make? I thought you hated the school and everyone in it. You will have the experience of studying in Russia. Not any of the other children are going to do that. You started kindergarten early, at my suggestion. You are a full year younger than any of the others. When we come back and you begin high school you will be the same age as everyone else," replied Gene. He straightened up from the last box and rubbed the small of his back.

"It doesn't matter how old I am! I wouldn't be friends with those creeps even if we were the same age. I'm not going to graduate here because we're leaving. And I'm not going to graduate from my old school with my friends because mom died. It all feels sad and awful. It doesn't matter anyway. Besides, I thought we were going to Russia for you?" Gina said in a matter of fact way. She did that whenever she didn't want to feel emotional. Gina looked at her uncle. She thought that for the first time he looked older and tired.

Gene slammed the roll of packing tape from his hands to the floor. He nearly shouted at her, "Gina, what do you expect me to do? You are unhappy and I don't know what to do for you! I thought your moving here would be good for you! I can't make anything work anymore. I have ruined your life. I have waited my entire career for a position like this. I am afraid I am hurting you by accepting." He kicked a packing box aside and walked back to the house.

Gina slammed her own roll of packing tape to the floor. She stomped after him into the house. "Well, I'm here and you're just going to have to admit that you haven't ruined my life. I am too young to have a ruined life! Mom would be mad at you! If we are going to Russia, I'll just have to make the best of it!" proclaimed Gina.

Gene sat down on the sofa and stared at the wall opposite. She surprised herself as she said to Gene, "It's about time you stop reading those dumb, depressing Russian novels and get on with life!"

He looked at her and said slowly, "Well, it would leave far fewer books for us to pack." He smiled and Gina sat down next to him.

"You know, I bet they have all of your books in Russia, anyway, you goof! Uncle Gene, we're having pizza and a Disney movie for tonight and that's that!" said Gina. She put her arm around his tired shoulder.

Gina pretended that the pizza was the best she had ever had. She pretended that seeing *Aladdin* again was great. Gene pretended the best he could, too, even though Gina had called him a goof. After the movie she said "Good Night" to Gene and went to her room. She cried everything out.

"I feel so awful. Nothing is fair! I hate leaving, but I don't want to stay. All I think of is mom and how much I miss her! Russia is so far away. I won't even have my kitty! I can't tell Uncle Gene. He's sad, too. I hate everything!" she thought. She sobbed herself to sleep.

"Russia? Russia! Oh, things are becoming ever so interesting!" Lily floated in circles above Gina's bed. The creases of worry in Gina's forehead slowly went away. Lily watched over Gina until she was sure she was dreaming sweet dreams.

Chapter Five

Gina was exhausted. The flight from Minnesota to New York's Kennedy airport was short and tiresome. The flight from New York to Helsinki, Finland was long and hard. She hadn't slept much. Gene was tense about the trip. He ran Gina through list after list, schedule after schedule.

Gene ticked off items in a small notebook. "We have dinner tonight on the plane. They will serve rolls and juice early tomorrow morning. We arrive in Helsinki at 8:10 a.m. If you are hungry at any time I have nuts and dried fruit."

"Yucko," thought Gina.

Gene continued, "The Leningrad flight leaves at 11:30 in the morning. We arrive in Leningrad at 1:30 p.m. We claim our bags and go through customs. We will be met by a man from the consulate named Harry at 2:30 in the afternoon."

"Gene, I'm really tired. Can't you tell me stuff right before it's going to happen?"

He looked up briefly from his notebook. "I want you to be prepared so you feel comfortable and not anxious regarding events of the trip."

Uncle Gene, I'm fine. Please be quiet. I'm going to sleep." He continued on silently, checking details in the notebook. Oh, her uncle could be irritating.

She was so unhappy. Nothing seemed right. Gina didn't think that moving to Russia would make it any better. Gina wanted to cry and sob and be desperately miserable, all at the same time. She couldn't. She couldn't let her uncle down. He was all she had now.

Gina woke up as she was being served dinner. After dinner she fell asleep again to dreams about Minneapolis. Gina dreamed about Aunt Maggie and Uncle Robert's wedding reception. She had been the flower girl in a long flower-print dress that she hated. She was escorted by a young cousin of Robert's. He was too shy to talk to her. She was too shy to talk to him. Gina also hated what the troops of smiling cousins, aunts and uncles said about her.

"That Gina, so odd and shy. Good thing she can dance!" Gina heard one of her distant cousins remark.

"She's not at all like Lily, is she? She must take after her father. He left them, didn't he? Good thing!" Gina heard a great-uncle say.

Gina felt as though she had been in detention for an entire day and night! She tried to be like everyone else. It was frightening to be stared at by so many people. She was only nine. Lily, matron-of-honor in her sister's wedding, smiled her lovely smile. She danced with everyone at the reception.

Gina woke up feeling ungraceful and clumsy. Lily loved to have people look at her. Lily lit up a stage like nobody's business. Gina wanted audiences to love her, too.

"I'm so mad at you, mom. How could you leave before you helped me get over stage fright? Everyone loved you. No one likes me. And no one likes my dancing. I hate being twelve. I hate moving. And I hate not wanting to do ballet anymore! I can't figure out why I don't want to dance!" she thought. She struggled to find a restful position in her confining seat.

Gina slept again and dreamed about her female cousins. There were three of them, all sisters. Every last one of them was attractive, lively, and blissfully normal. Aunt Maggie and Uncle Robert had adopted all three of them together. The twins were eleven and the little one was seven. They tried hard to accept and understand Gina. None of them wanted to study ballet. They played rousing games of touch football and soccer. They were mystified when Gina refused to play.

Gina dreamed that she was like them. She dreamed of her Aunt Maggie's house and being with all of her cousins. For once Gina got it right. She dressed like they dressed. She talked, smiled, and laughed like they did. They played soccer together. The cousins loved her back.

The dream ended like *Alice in Wonderland.* Gina climbed through secret passages and secret doorways. Places her cousins did not want to follow. Gina squeezed herself through one final tiny doorway. She ended up outside of their house on the grass. She ran away as fast as she could. She woke up knowing that she was different after all.

Gina stared out the plane window. Gina knew that there was something that set her apart from her cousins' warm, happy lives. Gina wondered if she could dance and be happy. Lily had been supremely happy dancing. Sometimes just the thought of performing made Gina feel green.

"Can't dancing and feeling great go together?" Gina asked herself as she fell into sleep once more. She awakened in time for breakfast in the air.

Pulkovo International Airport in Leningrad was not like any airport in America, Gina thought after they landed. That was for sure. It was made of grey cement. The people who worked there were grey, too. They did not smile or offer help with anything. Gene and Gina showed their tickets to the officials in baggage claim. They were ushered into the room where luggage from foreign countries was kept.

"Why isn't there anyone else here?" Gina asked her uncle.

"Our bags are kept separate to be checked. It is to protect Russia from foreigners bringing things in that are forbidden." Gene heaved one of the large suitcases they had packed onto a waiting cart.

"What's forbidden?" Gina asked adding her suitcase to the cart.

"Cigarettes, alcohol, the Bible, other things. It is also designed to keep Russians from stealing things from the bags of foreigners. We have many more products than the Russians do." Gene added another suitcase to the groaning cart.

"Why don't Russians just go to other places and buy stuff?" Gina asked. They peeked into the duty-free shops that held strange items for sale.

"Travel to other countries is difficult, expensive, and almost always not allowed. Russians are rarely allowed to leave Russia," Gene replied. Gina looked at ladies' fur coats, black caviar in round tins, and brightly colored stacking dolls. Other than blue and gold teacups, nothing else was in the shops.

“No one can leave? So, are we stuck here? They don’t even have t-shirts with ‘Leningrad Hard Rock Café.’ No plastic models of stuff, or even key chains. I’m not going to make it, Uncle Gene. We better go back.”

“Gina, you promised to try. We are allowed to leave if it is absolutely necessary because we have U.S. passports. The rest of Leningrad does not look like the airport.”

“What difference do our passports make?” Gina tried to help Gene push the heavy cart.

“It would be hard to explain right now. And we are both tired.” Gene pushed on the cart again, but it would not roll.

“Oh, all right. But everything is so complicated!” Gina bent down and straightened out one of the wheels on the cart. Gene was now able to push the cart to the customs area.

They went through customs. Gene responded to all of the official’s questions in Russian. He showed his work visa and their passports. They went off to meet Harry from the consulate. No travelers were rushing back and forth to catch planes or taxis or busses. It was dead and quiet. All Gina heard was the sound of her and her uncle’s footsteps on the hard floors of the concourse.

Gina was relieved when Harry arrived to greet them. He was from the U.S. consulate. Gene would work with Harry once they were settled. Harry was large, fifty years old, and smiled much. Gina liked him.

“Hello, Gina,” Harry said, as Gene introduced them. “I’ve worked at the consulate for ten years, now. You and your uncle are in good hands.”

“You’re not going to try to get me to learn Russian are you, Mr. Harry?” Gene smiled to himself.

Harry laughed, “No, of course not. And you can call me, ‘Harry.’ You’ll have plenty to do just getting used to living here. It’s not like the U.S.” Gina liked him more. “I do love Russia, but vacations are very necessary. I go home to the United States yearly. I go to Helsinki for the weekend every three months.” Harry helped Gene push the heavy cart.

"Harry, what do you do in Helsinki? We only were in the airport there. I didn't really see anything," Gina asked, walking next to them.

"Well, Gina, I buy foods that I like that I can't get here. I go to movies that are forbidden in Russia. I read books and magazines that are not allowed. I have as much fun as I can until I have to return to the dreariness of Leningrad." Harry was starting to puff from pushing the cart.

"Then why do you come back to Leningrad?" Gina decided to help push, too.

"It's an incredibly exciting time in the history of Russia. The potential jarring of the current regime..." Harry continued on about the changes in government.

In some ways he was like Uncle Gene. Gina cut him off. "Please Harry, stop. I don't know what regime means and I don't want to know. I don't want to know about the history, or whatever. I'm tired!"

The three waited outside the airport on the street with their bags. Harry hailed two cabs. Harry followed behind in the second cab with half of the luggage.

The driver took them to an apartment just off of Nevsky Avenue on Rubenstein Street. Nevsky Avenue was the large avenue that ran through downtown Leningrad. Rubinstein Street was far enough away to be quiet. They entered a large, beautiful courtyard. It was surrounded with arched columns that were as high as the top level of the buildings.

There were four buildings surrounding the courtyard. Harry paid for the cab rides and led them to number seventeen. It was lovely. Gina thought she might like their new home. Cats were frightened away by their approach. Several tabbies dashed to hide under the tiniest automobiles Gina had ever seen parked under the arches.

There was no elevator. They climbed to the fifth floor. The three huffed and puffed as they moved the heavy luggage slowly up the stairs. "Bet you're glad you decided not to bring all of those Russian novels with you. I am pretty sure they have all of your favorite titles here in Russia," Gina slyly said to Gene as they pulled and tugged the luggage up the final set of stairs.

"Yes, Gina, and I cannot thank you enough for reminding me of the fact. I did limit myself to bringing only my copy of *War and Peace,*" Gene assured her.

"*War and Peace?* Isn't that the longest book ever written?" joked Harry as Gina giggled. Gene found a tired smile to give to them. Harry unlocked a door that was upholstered in maroon leather. He then unlocked another wooden door inside of that.

They entered the narrow foyer. Gene and Gina followed Harry into the living room. It was covered in deep red wallpaper. The furniture was old-fashioned. Many of the boxes Gene and Gina packed had been delivered. They were stacked all over the room. A kitchen and dining room were off of a hallway to the right. Farther down the hall were two bedrooms and a study for her uncle. A bathroom and separate shower room were at the end of the hallway. The rooms were small, but not nearly as small as her uncle had warned her.

Her bedroom had wallpaper with purple pansies on a cream background. Her bed had a down feather comforter with a blue and white flowered sheet buttoned over it.

"What do you think, Gina?" asked Gene.

"It's pretty, Uncle Gene. I'm going to bed."

"Yes, both of you must be exhausted. Gene, a driver will be by for you in the morning," said Harry. He shook hands with Gene and they headed for the front door.

"Night, Harry. Night, Uncle Gene," Gina murmured as she went into her room. She was already asleep when Gene returned to check on her. Gina slept well her first night in a new bed in an old apartment in the center of Leningrad.

Lily tossed and turned in her corner of the ceiling. "I'm too excited to sleep! I can't believe I'm finally in Russia! Well, sort of here. In my own ghostly way, I guess. Sweet Gina. She is getting rest. This change is good for her." Lily blew her a kiss.

Chapter Six

Gina woke up. A stocky, red-haired, older woman was in her bedroom. She screamed and clutched her comforter around her neck. Gene came running.

"Gina, this is Valerya Isidorovna Petrovna. It slipped my mind to tell you about her on the way. She will be helping out around the house. She will cook for us."

"That whole long stupid list you had on the plane and you forgot to tell me about her?" Gina held the comforter closer around her neck.

"Yes, and I am sorry." Gene turned to the confused older woman. "Valerya Isidorovna, svoya plemyanitsa, Gina. Ana pa russki nee guvoreet." Gene turned back to his niece, "Gina, Valerya Isidorovna does not speak English." Gina and Valerya Isidorovna nodded at each other.

Valerya Isidorovna made her way to the kitchen.

"Uncle Gene, she doesn't speak English? Really? What did you say to her?"

Gene handed her a light grey and white striped cotton robe.

"I told her that you are my niece and that you do not speak Russian. You will be fine with her. Soon you will know some Russian."

Slipping the robe over her nightgown underneath the covers she tensely asked, "Fine? I bet she makes food I hate and I can't even tell her!"

Gene sat on the chair in front of her dressing table. "You have not yet tried anything that she has cooked. You might like it. I hired her on recommendation from the consulate. You must call her by her full first and second names, Valerya Isidorovna. Isidorovna is her second name which is Valerya's father's first name."

"What? There you go again! It's too confusing! I can't say all that. You are so crazy! Can't I just call her Valerie? Why do we have to drag her father into it?" Gina waved her hands excitedly in the air for emphasis.

"Because it is polite. It would be disrespectful to call her anything else. Let's practice. Say, 'Zdrastvooitye, Valerya Isidorovna.' That is how to say 'Hello' to Valerya Isidorovna properly."

Gina choked out something resembling what Gene asked her to say. He wrote the phrase down in English letters. Gina used it to study before she had to talk to Valerya Isidorovna again.

Gina looked up from her cheat sheet. "So that's why Russian novels are so long! They must need extra pages just to fit the names in!"

Gene smiled. "Gina, please have breakfast and then unpack your things. You can arrange your room anyway that suits you. I will be home in the early afternoon and continue to work from here. You will start attending school in a week."

"A week! We just got here! School sounds awful." Gina got out of bed and opened a packing box to look for clothes.

"Gina, you promised me that you would try." Gene patted her shoulder.

"All right, all right. See you later, Uncle Gene." She continued rummaging for any two pieces of clothing that even slightly matched one another. Gene left for the consulate.

Including all the names, it took Gina several tries just to say "Hello" to Valerya Isidorovna. Gina sat down to breakfast. She found that she liked the kasha and boiled eggs. Gina signaled by pointing down to the street that she would like to take a walk. Valerya Isidorovna put on a coat and directed Gina to do the same. She made Gina wear a scarf. Gina did not like it, but she wore it.

On the way to the park Valerya Isidorovna read the street signs out loud to her.

"Ulitsa Rubinshtayna?"

"Yes, Valerya Isidorovna. I know Rubinstein Street," Gina nodded.

"Nevsky Prospekt?"

"Yes, Valerya Isidorovna. I know Nevsky Avenue, too," Gina nodded.

They crossed the Naberezhnaya Reki Fontanki, one of the many canals in Leningrad. Valerya Isidorovna pointed out Karavannaya Street to their right. She said it so many times that Gina knew to repeat it back with the street part in Russian, "Karavannaya Ulitsa."

Valerya also said "Ekaterininskiy Skver," several times. Gina repeated it for her. Gina did not know that the square was named for tsaritsa, or Queen, Catherine the Great. There was a large monument representing Catherine in the square in the middle of a park. Gina didn't think that Catherine the Great was beautiful enough to have a monument made in her likeness. But she couldn't ask Valerya Isidorovna about it, because she didn't know enough Russian.

In the park Valerya Isidorovna sat on a parkbench and chatted with her friends. She explained wildly with her hands and in Russian that Gina was allowed to walk alone if she stayed very close by. She kept a watchful eye on Gina. Even so, the moment Gina was away from her she ripped the scarf off of her head.

Gina liked the delicious fear of taking a short walk. She looked at the street signs near the park. Valerya Isidorovna had just read them to her. At first she was not able to read the Russian letters on the street signs. Then Gina felt a thrill when she learned to read them herself. Gina remembered some of the things she had learned from her uncle's Russian lessons back in Minnesota.

Gina joined Valerya Isidorovna on the park bench. She nodded and smiled at the elderly lady's friends. She murmured "Zdrastvooitye" to them. Valerya Isidorovna put the scarf back on Gina's head. They started for home.

Gina decided not to mention to Gene that she was able to read the Russian letters on the street signs. She was afraid that he would give her more lessons. He had changed tactics anyway. Now he left Russian grammar books and dictionaries out around the apartment.

"He must think I'm an idiot. As if I didn't know what he's trying to do! Get me to study Russian!" she thought to herself. Often she looked up a new word or phrase that she learned from Valerya Isidorovna. Gina carefully replaced the books exactly as she found them. She congratulated herself that he would never know she was learning Russian. Gene couldn't start in again with his ridiculous quizzes!

After a few nights she found that she liked the down comforter and featherbed even more. She looked forward to slipping in between them. Lying in her bed at night, neon lights shone in from the street. She loved falling asleep surrounded by her purple pansy wallpaper. It reminded Gina of her bedroom in her mother's home in Minneapolis. One summer she and Lily had papered almost all of the walls in the house. Together they had chosen each lovely paper, a different one for each room.

Gene and Gina were invited out often those first few days in Leningrad. She enjoyed visiting the homes and summer-home dachas of her uncle's new colleagues. The swirl of tiny apartments, diplomats from the embassy, their children and wives were a blur to Gina. She was still getting used to being in a foreign land.

In each place that she visited, Gina found a beautiful surprise on every wall. And no two wallpapers were alike. Of all the places she visited, drank tea in, wore her Sunday dresses in, no two designs were the same. Gina knew Lily would have loved to see those beautiful wallpapers.

One night she was beginning to fall asleep. Gina dreamed the dream again. It was the dream that had kept her from peaceful sleep so many nights since her mother died. Gina dreamed that she was in her parents' house. In the dream she was in the basement. She was afraid. She climbed a secret staircase all the way up into the attic.

She found books about ballet in the attic. She found the bodice and tutu to a costume on an old headless dress form. She wanted to take the books and the costume with her. The books were very old and very large. Gina did not take the time to look at them. She was too afraid of something in the room to stay very long.

In the dream intense loneliness surrounded her. There was no comfort in the room. There was no sound, only silence. Everything was covered with a white dust and a white light. Gina felt so alone. The room was round, the walls curved and freezing cold. She saw her breath as she tried to breathe past her fear. She did not know what was frightening her.

Each time she dreamed this dream she made herself spend more and more time in the room. She tried the costume on. Gina was alone there, as if no one else in the world were alive. Gina awakened with a shiver. She wondered what the dream meant.

Lily watched Gina awaken frightened from her dream. She wished she could help Gina to be calm and sleep. "I suppose there are some things I have to let you figure out on your own, Gina. But I really don't like it when I can't help you! I may be a ghost, but I'm still a mother, after all."

Chapter Seven

In those first few days there were plenty of things to keep Gina from feeling lonely. There was the apartment on Rubinstein Street that she already loved. There were the gardens and parks. There were the teas and jams and other nice things that were served to eat in the afternoons.

The evening of the day before she was to begin school, Gina and Gene were having dinner. Gina asked, "Uncle Gene could I please, please take the trolley to school on my own? I've been on it enough with Valerya Isidorovna to do it."

"You may not. It is too dangerous. My driver will take you." Gene took a spoonful of his beet borscht soup.

"Uncle Gene, that's so embarrassing! The other kids will think I'm a snob."

"I can assure you that they are driven to school as well, Gina."

"What's going on that's so dangerous? Everything looks okay when I'm outside. This red soup is really good." Gina stirred sour cream into her soup and ate a spoonful.

Gene set his spoon on the table. "Have you noticed the large crowds outside the Kazan Cathedral?"

"Yeah, it's crazy, Uncle Gene. Valerya Isidorovna grabs my arm and practically makes me run past. But it's people dressed like clowns and jumping around, or people playing guitars and singing and dancing. Not scary things."

Gene looked at her with a serious face. "A young girl was attacked outside the Kazan last night. A week ago a man was murdered. The police are not doing much about it. In fact, they are pretending it never happened."

"That's awful! Why?" Gina was frightened.

Gene took a sip of water. "The people who gather at the Kazan are protesting the government. There are few jobs. There are shortages of food and gasoline. The people feel the government broke promises to give them jobs and food. Now they are angry.

The police are supposed to keep the protestors under control. Some of the police agree with the people protesting the government. It is not safe for you to be outside alone. You will ride with the driver."

"Okay. I guess I'll go pick out what I'm going to wear to school." "Ugh, school," she thought. Remembering her promise to her uncle to give it a try, she smiled as she went to her room.

The next morning after breakfast the car came to drive Gene and Gina. The driver would drop Gina at school and her uncle at the consulate. The driver would return for them in the afternoon. The driver's name was Timofei. Timofei was young, twenty-five years old. He was studying at the Foreign Languages Institute to be an English translator. He instantly asked that Gene and Gina call him "Tim." He liked the American sound. Gina knew she had found a friend.

He conversed with her uncle in Russian. She was surprised when he turned and asked Gina in English, "How do you like Leningrad?"

"I miss my cat, Tim."

"I am sorry to hear. Would you like new one?" Tim smiled and returned his eyes to the road.

From the back seat Gina leaned forward toward her uncle's ear. "Uncle Gene, remember you said we could adopt a kitten here?"

"I do. And I also remember you said that you would give the kitten back when we leave," Gene replied.

"Deal! Tim, do you know anyone who has a kitten I could take care of while we're here?"

"Not just now. I will ask friends," Tim responded.

Gina settled back into the seat. The seats in the car were covered in white muslin. Because of that Gina was afraid to touch anything. Tim had been hired as the consulate's chauffeur because he had connections. The gas shortage was severe. Tim had friends that helped him to get gasoline anytime day or night.

Gina was amazed at the string of people, places and deals that were needed to fill the gas tank. Gina watched Tim trade cigarettes for vodka. He drove to a different friend and traded vodka for champagne. He went on to a third friend and traded champagne for gasoline. The gasoline attendant knew that he could sell the champagne to foreigners for high prices. In return, he filled Tim's gas tank.

"Wow, Tim, all that just to get gas?" Gina was surprised.

"It is how we get along now. Times are difficult. No one knows if tomorrow government will change and we can get no more gas." Tim honked his horn as a taxi swooped close to them.

"Gina and I are grateful that you work with us, Tim," added Gene.

"Gene, I, too, am grateful to work for you. With you I can speak English. It is lucky for me to be with foreigners. Friends, they are jealous that you pay me with American dollars. I use dollars to buy electronic equipment. It is very difficult to get and expensive in rubles."

"I don't get the whole money thing," Gina said.

"American dollars are strong." Tim turned a corner so sharply they all lurched in their seats. "Sorry about that."

"Russian rubles are weak." Gene righted himself and returned papers and files to his briefcase that had popped open during the turn.

Gina handed some papers to her uncle that had flown into the back seat. "Well, I've never seen all of the money in the U.S. put together, or all the money in Russia put together. But people here don't dress like they do in the U.S. And they don't live in houses. Everyone lives in apartments. And not everyone has cars. I suppose that's what the weak and strong thing with money means."

Gina noticed that Valerya Isidorovna often wore the same clothing several times during the week. Driving through the city to her school, Gina looked out the window and noticed that her simple clothes were still far nicer than those of other girls her age on the street.

Gene clicked his briefcase shut. "That is probably the best way to look at the money system until you study a bit of economics. Look, there on the banks of the Neva River, the International School! It is housed in the ancient buildings of Leningrad State

University. Gina, this university is one of the oldest and most respected institutions in the world. While you are in class you can look across the river to the Winter Palace. Kings and queens lived there," Gene told her.

Gina frowned. "I bet they didn't have to go to this school. It looks old and creepy. The kings and queens got to hang out in the palace all the time. But, I will try, Uncle Gene."

Tim waited in the car while Gene took her around to meet her teachers. They all spoke English with the same Russian accent that Tim had. Gene left for the consulate. Gina went from class to class happy that no one tried to speak to her. Students had already formed groups of friends. That was okay with Gina. The others weren't interested in their classes. They spent most of the time trying to throw spitballs behind the teacher's back.

Gina confessed to herself that she didn't like the International School. The snobby American children of diplomats and businessmen were copies of the kids at St. Elizabeth's. The university buildings were chilly.

Gina was quiet when Tim and Gene came to pick her up.

"How did it go, Gina?" Gene took her books and helped her into the car.

"Well, Uncle Gene, the math class wasn't too awful. The food was okay. Those rooms are freezing!"

"I do remember the cold classrooms in the university. Everyone was nice to you?" Gene asked as Tim sped off into traffic.

"Yeah, it was okay." Gina's voice sounded tired.

Tim knew that the day had not gone very well. He tried to cheer Gina. "You know, I was not great in school. I only loved to talk and to dance."

"To dance?" Gene and Gina said in unison.

"I am ballroom dancer since five years old. I danced in competitions all over Russia. I dance waltz, foxtrot, tango, and Latin dances. Judges love my smile. And dancing, too, naturally." Tim slammed on his breaks to avoid rear-ending a car that had stopped suddenly in front of them. All three lurched forward and then back.

"You've been dancing for twenty years?" Gina saw that Gene had been ready with his briefcase this time. He clutched it to his chest and not one paper had fallen out.

"Gina, dancing is wonderful thing! Many children at age of five study ballroom dancing in Russia. I no longer compete. I only dance for fun."

Tim flipped down the sun visors on the windshield. He had stuck pictures of himself as an eight year-old boy in a tiny tuxedo with a number on his back. He was dancing with a little girl of similar age in a fluffy ball gown. They smiled up at the camera from the midst of a competition with thirty or forty other children. They all wore adult-style evening clothes.

"She now is my wife, Lena," he said as he pointed to the little girl.

"You met her when you were five!?" Gina was amazed.

"Yes, we fought all time," Tim laughed. "Then when we were twenty years old, she liked me. We married."

"Baby in other picture is our son, Misha." Tim pointed to a baby picture.

"Tim, the road!" Gene shouted as they narrowly missed a streetlamp.

Tim got back onto the street. "Oh, yes, of course. I am sorry." He continued, "And you know, we live near to you on Rubenstein Street. We are in fourth building, closer to Nevsky Avenue. And here you are, home."

Gene and Gina said "Good Night" to Tim. They had dinner. Gina did her homework. She went to bed. The next day she went to school and did it all over again. Tim's driving slightly improved. And in this way, Gina endured her first few weeks of school in Leningrad. In the apartment with Gene she pretended it was not so bad.

Gene loved to come and fetch her with Tim after school. He dropped in and chatted with his old professors from his university days. Gene picked up Gina at the International School and they walked to faculty offices of Leningrad State University. Gina learned to love the gentle old scholars who had instructed her uncle when he was young. They doted on her. They found out when she had study hall at the International School and came and took her out of class. She had cakes with them in their offices each afternoon at tea-time.

One afternoon Gene and Gina were visiting with the professors after school. One of the elderly professors, Viktor Fyodorovich, suggested, "Gene and Gina, I know ballet instructor who might take Gina as student."

"Gina, I think it may be time for you to return to ballet lessons," said Gene pouring her some tea.

"Uncle Gene, Viktor Fyodorovich, I don't know! I don't know if I could!" Gina cared even less about performing on stage now that Lily was gone. She didn't want to be bothered by some ballet teacher pushing her to dance on stage. Her pointe shoes gathered more dust in her closet.

"Would I have to perform on stage?" Gina asked anxiously.

"That will be wish of instructor. You not wish to dance in theater?" Victor Fyodorovich frowned in confusion.

"No, Viktor Fyodorovich. I don't. I love to dance! I just don't like to perform." Gina looked a little ashamed.

"A ballerina who not like to show self. This is unusual situation. I will mention to ballet instructor when I ask about lessons for you." He popped his third cake into his mouth and smiled at its sweet taste.

"Thank you, Viktor Fyodorovich!" Gina and Gene helped clear the tea things and they went out to meet Tim.

That evening after dinner Gene brought up the subject of ballet lessons. "Gina, I noticed you perked up at the talk of ballet lessons."

"I promise I'll think about it. I can't promise I'll do it. Good night, Uncle Gene."

"Spokoinoi nochi, Gina. It means that I wish you a calm, and peaceful night."

"Spokoinoi nochi, Uncle Gene. I can say it!" She said it over a few more times as she went down the hall to her room.

Lily perked up, too. "Oh Gina, I know you have to live your own life. I know I shouldn't want you to do things just because I never got to do them. But, this is a chance of a lifetime! To study ballet in Leningrad! Lily crossed her fingers and ankles. She even tried to cross her toes in hopes that Gina would decide to dance again.

Chapter Eight

One Sunday Gene hired Tim privately to drive them to the countryside. Tim's wife, Lena, and their baby son, Misha accompanied them. Gene sat in the front with Tim. Gina sat in the back with Lena and Misha. It cheered Gina to spend time with a little baby. He giggled and cooed as they jounced along the bumpy country roads. Lena knew some English, but not as much as Tim.

"Gene, I have music you will like. It is from George Gershwin." Tim was proud of the tape deck and his vast collection of American music. He popped in a tape.

"*An American in Paris!* Wonderful, Tim. This is marvelous music." Her uncle also liked ballroom music from the 1940's. Tim played that sometimes on the way to school in the morning.

"Tim, I need to hear M.C. Hammer!" Tim and Gina burst into song. *U Can't Touch This* floated out the open doors of the car. Gina nudged Gene in the back. He began snapping his fingers in time.

"Uncle Gene, Lena says that I can call her Lena. I don't have to say those other names like with Valerya Isidorovna. Isn't that great?"

"Yes, Gina, but it is important that you know how to address Valerya Isidorovna the proper way."

"This is true. We need always to show babushka respect," said Tim. He parked the car on the side of the road.

Everyone got out of the car. Each grabbed something for the picnic to take into the woods. "What's a babushka?"

"It means grandmother, Gina. You are a devushka, said Gene struggling with the heavy picnic basket. Tim took one end of it and they started looking for a level place to put down a blanket.

"So, I guess devushka means young girl," said Gina. She ran ahead to point out a good place in some shade.

Gene, Tim and Lena all said in unison, "Da!"

"And da means yes!" laughed Gina.

The picnic lunch was wonderful, Gina thought. Bread that was so good it didn't need butter, wonderful cheeses, pickles, and cold tea. After lunch Misha napped. Gina and Lena listened to Gene patiently helping Tim with his studies. The drive back was quieter. Tim put in a cassette of Astor Piazolla's tango music. Gina looked out at the thousands of birch trees as they flashed by outside. She thought about how a ballet piece could be choreographed to tango music. That reminded her of her mother. Gina turned her head more sharply toward the window as tears started.

She remembered being at home in her room in Minneapolis with her mother. She remembered Lily telling her that whenever she felt mad or sad she should dance. "But mom, that's when I dance the worst. I can't think straight. I can't remember the steps. I can't get the turns right. I just get frustrated. What's beautiful about that? It's awful."

Lily had told her, "Those emotional times are part of your training. Someday you will use it in performance."

Gina remembered how awful her first performance had been. Waiting in the wings, Gina had stage fright. She ran out and down the hall. She made it to the restroom in time to be sick. Gina resumed ballet lessons, but vowed never to dance on stage.

"Well, that was my stupid dancing career," thought Gina. She coughed and sneezed to cover up wiping her eyes with a tissue. Gina gave Tim and his family a weak smile when they reached the apartment. She and Gene said, "Good-bye." Gene put his arm around her shoulder as they climbed the stairs.

Later she dug the pointe shoes out of her closet. She sat on the edge of her bed holding them. She thought, "Maybe I can figure out how to not be afraid without mom." She carefully placed the pointe shoes on her nightstand.

Gina awakened the next morning. Her pointe shoes were on the pillow next to her. "That's funny. I know I put these on the nightstand."

Lily turned a pirouette in midair. "Oh, I suppose that was a little obvious. I hope it works!"

Chapter Nine

Gene and Gina spent time together in the evenings watching T.V. Gene liked to interpret for Gina as they watched movies and cartoons. Sometimes Gina found his translations annoying. But she let him do it. She saw how much he enjoyed telling her what the Russian words meant.

One evening, they heard a knock on the door. A tall fourteen year-old boy with large, brown, gentle eyes stood in the doorway.

"Hello. My name is Nikolai. I live in same building as Tim and Lena. I am here to return book. Tim borrowed from Dr. Shostek," he explained.

"Thank you. I'm Gina. Will you come in?" She opened the door wide.

"If it will be all right." The boy hesitated.

"Sure. Cookies?" Gina led him into the living room.

"Sounds great!" He sat down on the sofa.

Gina got tea and cookies from the kitchen. Her uncle was finishing a telephone call. It was one of the rare occasions when the telephone worked.

Gina set the tea tray on the coffee table. "Can I call you Nick? It's so much easier. Do you want milk or sugar?"

"No, I like without. And, call me Nick. It is good." He smiled.

Gina dumped some of both in her tea. "You speak English. How did you learn it? I think Russian is really hard."

Nick took his cup of tea from Gina. "Yes, my Aunt Tatiana is teacher of English Literature. She helped me to learn. I can help you to learn Russian if you like."

Gina bit into a wafer cookie. "No, thanks though. I have enough people teaching me Russian right now. It's kind of nice to have a break. What kind of stuff do you like to do?"

"I am very interested in computers. I am quite good in science, mathematics, and physics. I have great hopes for future of Russia. I am inventor," Nick told Gina.

"Wow. And you have to know math to do that?" Gina added more sugar to her tea.

"It helps." He smiled again.

Gina let him rattle on about his inventions. She knew that her uncle would love the young man. Gene hung up the phone and joined them.

"It is nice to meet you, Nick. Thank you for returning the book," Gene said. They shook hands. Gene took a cookie. Gina went off to get more tea. When she returned they were hunched over Gene's computer. They were deep into a discussion about gigs or bytes or something. Gina didn't know.

"Good night, you two!" Gina called out. She headed to her room. Gene and Nick looked up with glowing smiles. They wished her pleasant dreams.

Nick came over often in the evenings to discuss the entire universe with Gene. Gene was teaching him more about his computer. Gina came to understand Nick better. She looked forward to his visits. He spoke mainly to her uncle. One night Nick stayed over so late talking with Gene, that Nick's father came over to take him home.

"Uncle Gene, how come when Nick's father comes to pick him up he won't look at our faces?" Gina asked after they left. Gina watched out the window as the two made the way back to their apartment. The boy was chattering excitedly about all that he had learned. The old man trudged along beside him, head bent, shoulders caved in.

"He is an alcoholic, Gina. He can't feel joy or hope anymore. His body has given in to the disease. He is embarrassed that he can no longer control his own will. Alcoholism is quite a large problem in Russia. It is also in the U.S. Nick raised himself. It is as if he has no father at all," answered Gene carefully.

"You mean like with my dad?" asked Gina. She remembered a serious conversation her mother had with her about Gina's father.

"Yes, alcohol is a shroud that hides a man from all other people. No one can ever be more important to them than the desire to hide from the world," said Gene.

"You know, Uncle Gene, I'm glad I came to live with you. I mean it's still really hard, but you are so nice to me. And you watch out for me. Anyway, I'm glad I'm here. I'm glad you take care of me."

Gene put his arm around Gina's shoulder. "Thank you, Gina. I, too, am very glad that we are together. I rather like almost having a daughter." He had on his teaching armor and Gina didn't even care. She hugged him anyway.

"Why didn't you ever get married, Uncle Gene?" Gina sat on the sofa.

Gene fiddled with some magazines on the coffee table. "Oh, I was always traveling. Studying abroad. Working abroad. I had only started to settle at the university. Then the position here came up."

"And you never met the right girl." Gina looked at him thoughtfully.

"Yes, that too, I suppose." Gene smiled slightly.

Gina looked back at him over her shoulder on the way to her room. "Maybe you'll meet someone here. Maybe a ballerina!" Gina giggled.

The next Sunday morning Gina looked out into the courtyard. She spied a piece of flowered fabric moving in the bushes. She heard a girl's voice calling, "Sugarplum, Sugarplum!"

"Sugarplum!" Gina thought, "She must know English!" Gina flung open the door to the apartment. She raced down the five flights of stairs. Bursting into the courtyard she called out, "Hello, hello! Where are you?" She had lost sight of the flowered skirt in her flight downstairs.

Gina at last saw the piece of moving fabric again in the bushes. She tugged on it. Another girl whirled around in surprise and looked frightened. She straightened up and looked into Gina's eyes.

"Sugarplum, you were saying Sugarplum! You know English," Gina said, smiling.

"I do, some," answered the girl. She darted off after a kitten that came out from under the bushes. It scampered across the path. Both girls ran to and fro so many times trying to catch the frisky kitten they were dizzy. Gina finally caught her. All three tumbled into a ball on the grass, laughing.

"Why is her name Sugarplum?" asked Gina.

"They call her for role in famous ballet," she answered. They both shouted together, *The Nutcracker Fantasy*!"

And Gina went on, "How do you know English? What's your name?"

"Moment! Let us sit properly." The two girls untangled themselves and Sugarplum. Spreading their skirts beneath them they carefully sat down. Sugarplum fell asleep in Gina's lap.

"My mother is teacher of English. My father is artistic director of ballet company. They call me Valentina."

"Valentina! And you even look like a valentine!" Gina spoke excitedly.

"And how am I like valentine, as you say?" she asked.

"Because you look like a girl with red lips and dark, curly hair on a valentine card. I bet you have boys giving you flowers all the time. I bet they follow you home from school every day just dying to carry your books," Gina answered.

"There is no time for things of small importance to me. All days I am studying and dancing. I am talented, serious student," replied Valentina honestly.

"You dance! My mother danced! I dance! Well, I used to anyway," Gina confessed.

"You must be girl Nick was talking about. Nick is my cousin. He comes to visit your uncle. Yes?" Valentina asked her new friend.

"Nick is your cousin! He is very nice. My uncle likes him very much. I'm glad I met you! My name is Gina. Can I call you Tina?" Gina asked.

"It is deal!" said Tina and the girls shook hands.

Gina continued petting Sugarplum. "My mother always dreamed of studying ballet in the famous Kirov ballet school." "That is academy where I study! It is best ballet academy in world. I train to be professional ballerina. When I am older I will dance in Kirov Opera and Ballet Company. You and your mother must come to visit academy."

"Oh, Tina, I guess Nick didn't tell you. My mother died last year. I am living here with my uncle." Gina cradled Sugarplum in her arms.

Tina put her hand on Gina's shoulder. "Oh, dear Gina, I am so sorry. Nick did not tell." She smiled and said, "I think we become good friends, yes?"

Gina smiled. "Yes, I think so, too."

Chapter Ten

The two girls became good friends. They saw each other nearly every day. Often her uncle worked late at the consulate. On those days on the way home from school, Gina asked Tim to stop in front of the ballet academy. They picked up Tina and give her a ride to her apartment.

One day in the car, Tina said, "Gina, I have idea! Since I go to academy to become ballerina, you must go, too! You must audition for my father. He is Artistic Director of Kirov Academy and Company.

"Tina, I can't study at the Kirov! I've never studied in New York, only in Minneapolis. I'm not good enough. Besides I haven't had lessons in months. And my uncle's friends at the university gave him a name of someone I can study with," Gina confessed.

Tina countered with, "Sometimes, time that you do not practice makes you better dancer. Come, show few steps for papa. And forget other teacher. Academy is best! We shall go see him!"

"Now? Tina, I can't!"

"Sure you can, why not? Tim, next stop, Mariinsky Theater!" Tina directed Tim.

"Don't you mean the Kirov Opera and Ballet Theater? Is it the same as the Mariinsky Theater?" Gina asked in confusion.

"Some still call it that. Name soon will change to Mariinsky Theater again. Papa has office there, in small building near theater. There is small studio also. Nothing to fear!"

Tina looked excitedly out the window as they neared the building where her father worked. Gina gulped, "Oh, no. Auditioning for the director of the Kirov. Tina, I can't! I just can't!"

Tina grabbed Gina's hand. "I audition with you if you like. Will be fine."

Tim smiled and drove the rest of the way to the theater. "I shall wait. Come out same door when you are finished," he said to the girls. They climbed out of the car.

The girls entered the office building near the theater. They climbed the wooden staircase to the fourth floor. They quietly entered a studio where Ilya Alexandrovich Mikhailov was coaching a boy student who would soon graduate.

Tina whispered, "Soon student takes final exams at academy. Papa is helping him."

Ilya Alexandrovich was showing a step to demonstrate a particular technique to his student. Tina's father was small and white-haired. He had the grace of his daughter. His whole body moved and swayed when he executed the step. Gina thought it looked like he was merely playing with the music. The student thanked Ilya Alexandrovich. He bowed, and left. Tina introduced her father to Gina.

Gina didn't know if she should curtsy, bow, or shake hands. She stood uncertainly. It didn't matter. Ilya Alexandrovich hugged her. Boy, she was glad she had learned how to say names properly.

"Hello, Ilya Alexandrovich. I am very happy to meet you. Thank you for letting me audition." Gina hugged him back.

"Tina has told me much about you. You should be dancing. We will find right teacher for you. Now, show." He waved his hand to the center of the studio and sat in a wooden chair in front of the mirror.

Tina gave Gina a pair of canvas shoes to wear to audition. Gina and Tina performed the *Lilac Fairie Variation* from *Sleeping Beauty*. Gina was accepted as a student.

"That's it? I can study here? How can you tell from that little piece I danced if I am any good?" Gina asked Ilya Alexandrovich breathlessly.

"My dear, I could tell from moment you put shoes on feet. It was as though you were greeting old friend," the elderly man answered. "You have trained with Branitskaya, yes?" he asked.

"She was my teacher in Minneapolis! How did you know that? When I turned ten, my mom got me an audition for Madame Lirena Branitskaya. She danced with the Bolshoi Ballet Company here before she moved to Minneapolis."

Ilya Alexandrovich smiled at her. "She has trained you to dance like her. I saw when you walked in door. Lirena and I are old friends, my dear. She was beautiful prima ballerina. I remember when she moved to U.S. I was very sad."

"I know I was lucky to be one of Madame Branitskaya's students. I loved her and I miss her, too. I took lessons six days a week and practiced at home every day."

Tina smiled and nodded at her father, "So, you see, papa, Gina needs to be with us."

"Gina, dear, why have you not been dancing?" Ilya Alexandrovich asked as he put a hand on her shoulder.

"I am not like my mother. My mom had a spark that made her different from everyone else. She made other people happy with her talent. I'm not talented. I'm boring on stage," Gina slowly answered. Ilya Alexandrovich and Tina smiled and lightly laughed. "What's so funny?" Gina demanded.

"Number one, you are not like mother, you are you, and no one else," Ilya Alexandrovich whispered to her as though telling her a big secret.

"And number two, talent and extra spark? They are hard work only. All can have who work hard enough!" said Tina as she spun circles across the room.

The girls smiled and said, "Good-bye." They clambered down the creaky wooden stairs. Gina chattered all the way home to Tina about dancing again. Tina hugged her as they parted. She went to the Mikhailov's apartment that was in the building across the courtyard from the Shosteks.'

Gina raced up the stairs and into the apartment. Gene listened as Gina breathlessly told him about the academy.

"Uncle Gene, I was there! I was at the Kirov School! I met Tina's father. A top level student was practicing. He did the hardest steps I've ever seen! And he was so good! Ilya Alexandrovich is so kind. And he knows everything about ballet. I wasn't scared at all. Tina was there with me."

"How did this come about?" Gene looked up from his newspaper.

"Tina said that she had been thinking about it. She just decided we should do it together. She told Tim to drive us to the Mariinsky

Theater. Did you know it used to be called that? Now it's the Kirov. They might change it back!" Gina skipped around the room.

"I do recall hearing something like that," Gene said with a smile.

Gina stopped skipping and announced. "So he watched me dance. He told me that I stand wrong. He made a correction to my spine. Then he said that I should begin in Level III in the International Division! At the Kirov Academy next Monday!"

Gene set down the newspaper and continued smiling. "Uncle Gene, can I study there? I mean, can we afford it?" Gina asked excitedly. "I don't know how much money you make over here and everything. It seems like we're doing okay. I think it'll cost more than my lessons at home. It's the Kirov!" Almost before she finished telling him, Gene was on the telephone to the Mikhailovs.' He arranged payment for Gina's lessons. He confirmed that Tim would drop her off at the academy at the appointed time on Monday.

Gina danced into her room. She started practicing. "This is my second chance. I'm going to figure out what I'm afraid of. Or figure out how to have courage. Or whatever I need to be a great dancer! I know I can do it, mom!" Gina vowed. She launched into one of the most difficult pieces she knew.

Lily danced her own joyous jig on the ceiling.

Chapter Eleven

This was what her mother had wanted to see, this long yellow building on Theater Street, the Kirov Ballet School. Gina remembered a book of her mother's called *The Children of Theater Street.* It was about this academy, the most famous ballet school in the world. The academy was over one hundred years old.

Anna Pavlova, Vaslav Nijinsky, George Balanchine, Rudolph Nureyev, Mikhail Baryshnikov, all had studied there.

"Tina, something's wrong," Gina whispered to Tina. They passed through the wooden outer doors. They went on into the square lobby. There was a picture of the famous teacher, Agrippina Vaganova, on the wall. All was quiet except for the occasional sound of a child's slippered feet scurrying down a hall or a muffled bit of girlish laughter.

Tina shushed her. She handed the woman who sat at the desk a permission slip from her teacher. Foreign visitors were rarely allowed to watch classes at the academy. The woman carefully placed the slip of paper under the glass top of the desk. She waved them through into the hallway.

Gina had been accepted as a student in the International Division. She was not allowed to take lessons with Tina in the Russian Division. Today Gina was to watch Tina's Level IV lesson. Tomorrow she would be allowed to study in the International Division Level III class. The International students were kept separate from the academy students that lived in Russia. International students were rarely invited to join the Kirov ballet company.

Most returned home to dance in companies in their home country. Russian students who did not live in Leningrad left their families at the age of nine or ten to live at the academy.

They left the woman at the desk and started down a hallway. Tina whispered to Gina, "What did you say before about something being wrong?

Gina followed closely behind. "It's not on Theater Street. Did the names of the streets change? And why are we whispering?"

"Academy is serious place for learning, that is why we whisper! Gina, there is no Theater Street. No, it has always been on Rossi and Zodchevo Streets. Kirov Theater, the one that used to be called Mariinsky Theater, is in Theater Square. Do you mean that?" said Tina.

"No. The book, my mother's book, *The Children of Theater Street*, said the academy was on Theater Street. That's funny. I guess the writers thought it sounded better to have the academy be on Theater Street."

"Americans are so weird," smiled Tina.

"We are not! Well, maybe a little. And why do you keep saying that the theater used to be called the Mariinsky Theater and soon will be called that again? Kirov Theater is so much easier to say. And to spell!" asked Gina. She followed Tina to the dressing rooms.

"Gina, I cannot explain. It is complex. Maybe your uncle and my papa can help you to know. Russia is changing now. That is all I understand. Enough! We are here to study ballet!"

Gina tried hard to look at the academy through her mother's eyes. The floors were wooden and old. The paint was chipped, either light blue-green or pale mustard yellow. The lights were dim.

"Ick," Gina thought. "They must have been having a paint sale."

Children ran through the halls in flimsy, cotton bathrobes and fuzzy bedroom slippers that covered their leotards and tights. Gina felt like she had interrupted a pajama party of girls who were light as butterflies. She waited in the changing room.

Tina hurriedly put on pink tights, a dull black leotard, white canvas shoes with white ribbons that tied around her ankles, and a robe. She put slippers on right over the ballet shoes. Gina glanced at the other girls quickly dressing. She wondered why there was little joking or giggling.

"Tina, why doesn't anyone smile here?" Gina whispered. Tina put her hair up into a neat bun. Neat for Tina anyway, who could rarely keep little curly, wispy pieces of hair from flying into her face while she was dancing.

"Gina, it is academy. Would you make fun and run around like clown at School of American Ballet in New York?" Tina asked.

"Okay, okay, I get it. How come the little girls wear white leotards and no tights and little ankle socks?" asked Gina.

"The little girls in first level dress that way. They are not allowed to wear tights. Then muscles in legs can be seen. I'm in fourth level so I wear black leotard and pink tights.

That is what upper levels wear. Top level, eighth level, wears whatever they want. Except on examination days, then they wear black and pink, too," Tina explained. She tried to plaster down the wisps with water.

"Things aren't this strict in Minneapolis! How many levels are there?" Gina asked.

"Eight, plus Zero Level," answered Tina.

"Zero Level! Who'd want to be in that? How do girls get picked to go to the school in the first place?" Gina wondered.

"Many want to be in Zero Level, silly. It is class for students too young to be in Level One. They are students commission thinks will be able to be in Level One next year. Commission decides who may come to academy. Commission is director of school, highest level teachers, and medical doctor." Tina continued plastering her hair down with water.

"What do the girls have to do to audition?" Gina sat on a long bench in the dressing room.

"Each girl must walk in front of commission in underpants. She must dance few steps. Then doctor looks at how flexible she is. Pedagogues ask her questions to know if she has right personality for dancer. She must be bright, hard working, able to remember what is taught to her, and have good feeling about life. So many questions. Come, we must hurry!" said Tina.

She grabbed Gina's hand and they raced down the hall to class. They ran off down the hall with the rest of the girls and into a pale blue studio. It had rounded windows and a slanted wooden floor.

Gina noticed that the studios were named for famous dancers who had attended the academy. Gina recognized their names because her mother had told her about them. There were signs outside the doors that read Nijinsky Studio or Pavlova Studio.

They were in the Nureyev Studio. The ceilings were very high. There were mirrors on one entire wall. Wooden barres to hang onto ran around the other three walls of the room. The girls busily sprinkled the floors with water out of a tin watering can so their shoes would not slip. Tina took Gina to a folding wooden chair near the piano.

"Sit here. Do not say one word. Stand up when teacher enters. Stand up at end of class stand also. Do not walk out of room before she does. Never stand in front of her!" Tina directed. Gina saluted her friend and silently sat down.

A woman entered and Gina rose as she was told. Tina came back over to Gina. "Not to her," Tina grinned. "She is pianist."

"We dance to a stereo at home. You have your own piano player, wow. Well, when is the teacher coming? We raced around like crazy. Now we've been waiting for ten minutes. Why did we rush?" asked Gina logically.

"Class starts at nine-thirty, but Lyudmila Valentinovna is never on time. Not any of teachers are. We hurry in case one day they decide to begin on time," Tina explained. She returned to the girls stretching at the barre and stretched herself. One girl took a watering can and sprinkled the wooden floor with more water.

Gina frowned slightly. She sat back down, only to stand up again as the delinquent Lyudmila Valentinovna arrived. As she entered, the girls immediately formed a half circle in the center of the room. They curtseyed twice in choreographed unison to their teacher. They waited for her to tell them they could take their place at the barre. The girls went to assigned places at the barre. The lesson began.

Tina had told Gina that the whole two-hour class was taught once a week on Mondays. For the remainder of the week the girls were expected to remember exactly all of the combinations. They must be able to execute them without asking questions or wondering what came next. Gina thought that was pretty amazing. At home Madame Branitskaya had demonstrated each and every combination every day.

Gina watched exercise after exercise. Girls executed the exercises with solemn faces and legs that stretched to elastic infinity. The pianist pounded out one uninspired, evenly counted tune after another. The girls performed each exercise starting with their left hand holding onto a wooden barre. The barre was slightly higher than their waist. They worked their right arm and leg. Then the students turned around and did the same exercise with their right hand on the barre. They used their left leg and arm.

"This is like with Madame Branitskaya, except everything is done much more slowly," thought Gina. Every few minutes or so Lyudmila Valentinovna stood up with an angry face. She sharply scolded the girls.

She asked a girl to do a step over and over. The little girl's eyed welled with large tears that eventually spilled over onto her cheeks and made their way down onto her leotard. After a few seconds the tears stopped. The girl did the step as her teacher wanted. She received a smile and praise in return.

After forty-five minutes the girls left the barre. They arranged themselves in evenly spaced rows in the middle of the room facing the mirror. For another forty-five minutes they danced slow balancing movements. They spun many pirouettes. The young ballerinas then jumped sautés.' Gina knew a ballet lesson had little resemblance to the dancing audiences see on stage. The daily work prepared a ballerina to be able to dance choreography that she performed in the theater.

The girls went over to a corner of the room. They changed into hard, pink pointe shoes. Gina and Tina loved those shoes. It did hurt to dance in those shoes sometimes. It was so fun to turn pirouettes in them when it didn't hurt. It was worth it. The girls formed rows again. For another half an hour they performed jerky movements wearing pointe shoes. Gina knew that to dance on pointe was difficult. It took many years of hard work to make the movements look graceful and beautiful.

The lesson was over. The girls curtsied twice to their teacher again. They thanked her as she left the room. Gina and Tina walked silently back down the hall. Tina changed clothes again. The girls went back out onto the street.

"What is matter, Gina?" asked Tina. They entered the park surrounded by a high black iron fence that held the monument to Catherine the Great. They were headed toward Nevsky Avenue. Tim was waiting nearby in the car. Gene had decided that it was safe enough for the girls to walk through the park as long as Tim was there waiting on the other side for them.

"Nothing. It's just, well, you weren't like I expected you to be," carefully answered Gina. "You were so calm in your dancing. You didn't show off, not one little bit. That girl who could lift her legs up to the ceiling practically pushed you out of the way. Why did you let her?"

"Because I am in class to learn. I must be quiet inside to let everything new inside of me. Papa taught me to do." Tina carefully skipped over each crack in the cement path. "But what about all of the emotional stuff that my mom kept telling me to do? Don't you have to do that?" Gina demanded.

"That is for stage," Tina said.

"Sometimes I could just scream!" Gina exclaimed.

"And why not? It might be good for you!" laughed Tina.

Gina laughed. "Maybe it's true." She started hopping over the cracks in the pavement, too. " My mother was like you in class. In real life she blended in with the woodwork, she said. She said she did that on purpose so she could watch other people and learn from them. Even if they were walking down the street she said that she could learn dancing from them."

"I think your mother was real first class ballerina," remarked Tina.

"I wish I could feel like a first class ballerina, even just once," said Gina. She told Tina her terrible secret about getting sick at her first recital. "As soon as I started earning money baby-sitting, I paid for lessons with Madame Branitskaya. My mom bought shoes, tights, and leotards. I wish she could've given me courage, too.

"I think maybe you have more courage than you know, Gina," suggested Tina.

"What do you mean?" asked Gina.

"Think, if you love self and think you dance great, maybe you would keep doing same steps over and over to stay that way, yes?" asked Tina. "You to say, 'I am not happy with self. I have to work harder.' It is your way to say, 'I want to learn more. I am not perfect, but I am becoming great ballerina.'"

"It all seems so easy for everybody else, Tina." Gina stopped skipping and was balancing on one leg.

Tina stopped skipping, too, balancing one one leg. "Fright of stage will leave when you are ready, Gina. Many girls here become sick before performance, or before examination. They are afraid they will be asked to leave academy if not dance perfect. They learn to dance better and sickness leaves! I have seen it many times happen!" Tina grabbed Gina's hand and tried to push her over. They laughed and continued skipping over the cracks holding hands.

Gina thought, "Mom, I wish I could tell you this stuff. Then you'll know I can be happy. I guess you're always happy, huh? Being in heaven and all." "Tina, why was the teacher yelling at that one girl? What was she saying?" asked Gina.

"Lyudmila Valentinovna yells that she did steps wrong. That is Katya. Her body not good for ballet. The teacher makes her work harder. She knows she may not pass examination," replied Tina.

"You all look perfect and exactly like each other. How can she be bad?" asked Gina in confusion.

"She is not bad. You know for self, Gina, that to study classical art is never to be perfect. She yells because she loves Katya. Lyudmila Valentinovna wants her to do well, though she has short, not elastic legs. Katya feels music and can tell story with emotions. One cannot study or perform ballet without strong emotion," explained Tina.

"First you tell me not to be emotional in class, then you say you can't study dance without it! I'm sick and tired of all of this emotion stuff! I never want to be yelled at or yell at anyone else! I dance just fine without someone yelling and screaming. And I will never, ever cry in front of other people!" Gina shouted.

"And this you scream to me!" noted Tina.

"I'm just excited about what I'm talking about. I'm not screaming. I just want you to know how important this is to me!" exclaimed Gina.

"Gina, Gina, my dear, it is pity that you do not look more often in mirror," said Tina.

Gina decided that she would ask later what Tina meant by the mirror remark. They ran through the park around the monument to Catherine the Great. By that time Tim had parked the car and come to find them. He yelled at them to get inside. They raced to the car. Gina won, but Tina said she let her.

Chapter Twelve

Gina had daily ballet lessons at the academy after school. There were five other students in the Level III International Division. The girls were from Japan. They knew some English, but not enough to chat with Gina. Gina liked the girls. They were quiet and worked very hard. They were kind to each other and to Gina.

One day a ribbon came loose on her shoe. Gina needed to do a fast sewing repair before class. She found she had forgotten to bring a needle and thread. One of the girls shyly came up to Gina. She showed Gina the needle and thread inside of her dance bag. Gina smiled. She used them to quickly sew her shoe. Gina nodded thanks many times to the girl. The girl nodded back and replaced the sewing items in her bag. Gina smiled again. The dance bag had a picture of Mickey Mouse on it.

The girls and Gina worked out a routine for sprinkling the floor with water from the watering can. It had to be done twice, once when the girls first arrived, and again after barre work was done. The water soaked into the ancient wooden floors and softened them. Then the girls did not slip as they danced.

Gina usually did the first round of watering because Tim dropped her off a little early each day. The other girls did the second round. They ran in each day from one of their academic classes at the academy. Russian was difficult for them, as it was for Gina. They stayed after class to ask for extra help with their schoolwork.

Several weeks went by. Ilya Alexandrovich dropped by Gina's class on occasion to watch her dance. Gina was surprised that she liked it when he visited. She thought it would make her nervous, but it didn't. He caused a stir when he came into the studio. As in Tina's class, the girls had been trained to stop what they were doing whenever a teacher entered the room. The girls formed a semi-circle and curtseyed twice to Ilya Alexandrovich.

After watching Gina's lesson, Ilya Alexandrovich escorted her and Tina out to Tim's car. Any students that they passed in the hallways, stopped and curtsied twice to Ilya Alexandrovich. The boys bowed twice, instead of curtseying.

One day after her lesson she and Ilya Alexandrovich were walking down the hallway to meet Tina.

"Gina, I need you to do something for me," he said, putting a hand on her shoulder.

Gina looked up at him. "Yes, Ilya Alexandrovich. What is it?"

"Tomorrow, after class find empty studio. Sit alone in room with pointe shoes. Do not dance. Look at shoes until you feel music calling you to dance," he instructed.

Gina uncertainly asked, "What? How long should I sit there? What music will I hear? I'll be alone."

"Music finds you," Ilya Alexandrovich said. "You do not find it. You are here to dance to music that already exists."

"Well, of course I do, " Gina replied. "I hear the music as it is played. I dance the steps that I have been taught."

He smiled. "It is much more than that, my dear. Music is all around us, everywhere, even music that no one has yet committed to notes."

"Tomorrow I'll try, Ilya Alexandrovich."

"Not try, DO," he insisted. Gina nodded. Tina skipped up to them and they went out to Tim and the car.

The following afternoon, alone, she entered one of the light, corner studios at the academy. She carefully set her pointe shoes on the floor about ten feet away from her. She sat in a wooden chair opposite. She looked, stared, and shifted. She gazed about the room. She studied her fingernails. She mentally rehearsed every dance she knew by heart.

Finally she decided that all of this was pretty silly. Maybe she didn't have talent, or genius, or sensitivity, or whatever it took to be a great ballerina. Gina had never wanted to be a great ballerina, she argued with herself. She only wanted to be a very good ballerina. Oh, darn it all, she did want to be a great ballerina. She sighed dejectedly. She rose to get a drink of water from the hall.

As her fingers touched the door handle she found herself turning around. She looked back at her shoes. They were a new brand and her favorite so far. Each time she had grown, or whenever her shoes were too soft to dance in, her mother had taken her to be fitted for new pointe shoes.

These were different. In them she had learned for the first time to understand phrasing of music. She learned to understand the many ways that the same choreography could be danced by different people. She couldn't leave them alone in a room without her. They were her closest friends.

She picked them up. As she drew them on and tied the ribbons, in her imagination, she heard music. Silvery high notes, golden deeper tones all came from somewhere far away. Gina wasn't dancing steps to music that she could hear. The shoes were remembering them from someone else who had danced and left them for her to find.

When the girls were in Tina's apartment after school the next day, Gina told her about her grand discovery with music.

"Oh, did Papa do that one to you?" Tina smiled knowingly. "Papa is wizard. He knows that you need to learn magic and that there is no magic without hard work. Povtoreniye, mat uchenia," explained Tina.

"Repetition is the mother of learning." How many times had Gina heard her uncle say that? "That is exactly how I think about dancing! Why did your father teach me that it is a magical, mysterious thing?" asked Gina.

"Because it is," replied Tina. "It is necessary to know both ways, hard work and magic."

Here we go again, thought Gina. Another one of those big secrets that all other artists seemed to have been let in on, except Gina. "The magic, what is it exactly?" she asked Tina.

"Mmmm, it is... It is...it is as I dance I do not feel that I am dancing. I think not of the role of my character. I think not of muscles or body. I am like feather flying in music," Tina struggled to explain.

"How can you not know that you are dancing? How can you remember what comes next if you don't know what you are doing?" Gina fervently asked.

"It is not thinking. It is not feeling. I know all and I am not working. I exist only," said Tina.

"But I thought it was all about hard work!" Gina became angry in her frustration.

"Yes, it is true. Hard work and then to fly. Then to come back, work hard and fly again. That is only what I can say," answered Tina. She smiled at Gina. Tina wanted her new friend to understand.

"How can I fly when I want, like I did in the studio yesterday afternoon? It was like you said, but I don't know if I can do it again! What if I never dance that way again? What if I spend my whole life dancing and it never, ever happens again?!" Gina was frightened now.

"Work hard and remember that afternoon. Remember the voice of papa. Remember the feeling to you. It will happen to you many times. I feel it will be," Tina gently instructed Gina.

The girls were in the Mikhailov's apartment playing with Sugarplum, and her older brother, Romeo, in the living room. Sugarplum followed Gina. She was always at Gina's side when the girls were in the Mikhailovs' apartment.

Tina shyly looked at Gina. "Gina, I am happy if you take Sugarplum home with you to live. She has chosen you, Gina. She wants you as friend."

"I'd love to take Sugarplum! But I have to give her back to you when we go back to the U.S. or Nijinsky will be jealous," explained Gina.

"That is good. Romeo and I are happy to do it!" said Tina. She smiled at her friend's happiness in receiving Sugarplum as a gift.

Chapter Thirteen

After school, ballet lessons, and homework, the girls often visited Tina's grandmother in the zagorod. The zagorod was the Russian countryside. It was a ways out from the city. Berries grew alongside the rough and bumpy roads. People tried to live life unaware of the mounting political chaos in Leningrad.

They took the subway to get to the train station. From there they would ride in a real train to get to the grandparent's house. It was the middle of the day. Gene had allowed the two girls to take the subway and the train instead of having Tim drive them. The subway stations were beautiful. They were full of graceful arches and sculpture, like in museums. Tina and Gina rode the escalator deep into the earth to get down to the subway platforms.

"Why did they build the subway so deep into the ground?" Gina faced Tina and rode backward on the moving stairs.

"They also can be bomb shelters if there is war. Longest ride is three full minutes on escalator." Tina made Gina turn around and ride the right way.

Once at the bottom the girls went to the platform to wait for their train. The subway trains stopped every few minutes to let riders off and on. The trains were very crowded. Often passengers waited until several trains passed by until one arrived that had room to let a new person inside. Once inside the subway train, it was frighteningly close. People pressed so near to Gina that she could not stand it.

"Tina, I hate this," Gina whispered.

"I know, only two stops." Tina tried to move away from Gina and make more room for her, but she was pressed right back where she had been.

"How can you stand having people so close to you?" Gina scrunched up her shoulders and made herself as small as possible.

"We are used to it. It is very big city, Gina. It is normal. Here is our stop." The girls squeezed themselves hard to get out of the doors and almost fell onto the platform.

Gina and Tina helped an elderly woman make her way through the sweeping crowds to the escalator. They helped her safely out onto the street. She thanked the girls over and over. She said that they were children of the past. She said that people used to help each other. They did not push and shove and think only of themselves. Tina translated for Gina. They waved "Good-bye" and headed for the above ground train platform.

On the forty-five minute train ride Gina had time to ask Tina about things she noticed in the city that didn't seem right. "Tina, in the shops I saw women buying baby formula. The mothers had to show identification to the clerk. Why do they have to do that?"

"Mothers have to show document to prove they live in neighborhood near store. It is awful Gina, but some times people come from other towns. They go into stores and by all baby food. They return to their hometown and sell there for high prices."

Gina looked sad for a moment. "Why don't they have baby food in all of the towns?"

"I don't know all, but I know it is because trains and trucks are not working to transport food. I don't know if there is not fuel for trucks, maybe? So, if there is babyfood factory in town, the baby food stays there. Other towns not get any." Tina said.

"That is awful!" Gina thought of helpless babies and mothers not able to get the right kind of food for their children.

Tina nodded. "It is. Last week I saw young man and elderly woman screaming on street. They were arguing over who was next in line for butcher shop. Line stretched on for blocks! Meat from farms is not being transported to shops in city. Coffee, matches, alcohol, sugar, coins for subway, and paper, all are shortages. Papa must go out very early to buy newspaper. By eight o'clock newspapers are sold out. People pass newspapers from friend to friend until they are read to rags."

"Why are there shortages of sugar?"

"Because of vodka. President Gorbachev made law that people could only buy two bottles on one day."

"What does that have to do with sugar?" Gina was completely confused.

"People have great stockpiles of sugar in homes. Some use for making vodka. People who don't make vodka, are afraid vodka makers will buy up all sugar. So, both kinds of people buy bags and bags of sugar whenever it is in stores."

"If you want to bake cookies and need to borrow a cup of sugar you ask a friend who makes vodka?" laughed Gina.

"Yes, and if you need to make vodka you ask friend who makes cakes!" Tina smiled.

"Tina, I have seen drunk men on the streets. They weave back and forth like they are going to fall."

"It is very big problem here. In evening police go around city. They pick men up and put them in jail. There they have food and warm place for night."

Gina wondered if her father had behaved like those men did in front of Lily. Somewhere inside of her, Gina knew that he had. She remembered once the police bringing her father home. She pretended to be asleep. She saw the police car lights outside her window. After the police left she heard furniture bumped around, a slap, and her mother crying. In the morning at breakfast no one said a word about what happened the night before. Gina was too frightened to ask. Gina realized what Nick's life might be like. It might be sad and full of pain.

Gina settled back into the dark green upholstered seat. Their train rattled on back and forth. The girls reached the countryside. The train was roomy and she could see out the windows. Life in the country was different from city life. Gina saw elderly men and women cutting grass and weeds by swinging curved knife-like scythes. There were no lawnmowers in the zagorod. Women wore scarves on their heads. The men wore hats.

The houses that flashed by were small wooden boxes weathered grey by rain and snow. The train made several stops at other small towns. Whistles blew at each station. Gina was worried that Tina would forget where to get off. She slept the whole way.

In the city, Gina saw that people often slept on the trains, busses, and subways.

They enjoyed a catnap before had to go back into the noise and bustle of the city. Tina opened her eyes as they pulled into the train station where her grandmother lived.

Tina's grandmother's house was like a house in the U.S., Gina thought, except from a long time ago. There was a narrow path that led up to a tiny white house. It was surrounded by a delicate, dark green lattice fence. The doors had curly carvings. All of the wood inside of the house was curved, too. European laces covered all of the windows and tables. The house had been a dacha, a summer cabin. The Mikhailov's decided to live in the pretty little house once they became too old to want to live in Leningrad.

The gardens were filled with herbs and flowers. The area around the house was tangled and overgrown. In the house, Gina felt like she was inside of a greeting card. A greeting card for someone who was sick and the drawing of the house was meant to cheer them up.

Gina was excited about the reason for their journey. They were going to celebrate Ilya Alexandrovich's birthday. Gene would arrive later after he finished work. Ballerinas and instructors from the Kirov ballet school, a painter, several writers, and half a dozen musicians would also be at the party. Tina's mother, Tatiana Ivanovna, and Nick would also be there. Tina and Gina helped Tina's grandmother until everyone arrived.

The girls cut and chopped vegetables for hours. Russians love their salads cut very finely. "I could have read *War and Peace* in the time it took to chop up all of this stuff," Gina thought. She rubbed her sore arms and hands.

The guests arrived. Gina hugged her uncle and Ilya Alexandrovich when they came through the door. Tim was there, too, having driven Gene. Each guest removed his or her shoes. They replaced them with a pair of the many slippers crowding the foyer.

The guests were seated. Tina's grandmother and the girls served a salad of carrots and apples. This was followed by orange caviar, and butter on bread. Gina tried it and admitted that she liked salty fish eggs. Then they had red beet borsht soup. Fish came next, and chicken with rice. Cakes and cookies were for dessert with tea or coffee.

There was wine throughout the meal. None was offered to anyone under the legal age. Gina sat between Nick and Tina.

"Usually we have champagne at celebrations. It is hard to get champagne now. There are new government taxes. Champagne makers are angry. They destroyed large parts of vineyards. They made less champagne. They sell only for high prices on black market," said Tina.

"Black market?" asked Gina.

"Gina, perhaps it is better not to explain tonight. It is party!" Gina was grateful. She probably wouldn't understand what a black market was anyway. Gina noticed that there was only enough food to go around. Not much was left over. Even so, the hostess asked who would like seconds. Everyone said that the food had been wonderful. Then they politely refused to accept seconds that didn't exist.

Gina didn't understand much when the conversation turned political. Suddenly, three of the men were slugging each other like hockey players. The women snatched the china from the table. They took the pictures off of the walls. The remaining men broke up the fight. Things settled down. The guests prepared to leave. Tina and her family were spending the night. Gene and Gina said "Good-bye" and got into the car with Tim.

Once they were on the road, Gina asked her uncle, "What the heck was that fight all about?"

"It was about President Gorbachev, Gina. He is hated because the people have no food. He is going to let the countries that made up a large part of Russia leave the union. They will become independent countries and have their own power. Much of the food and oil that supports the people in Russia comes from those countries."

"Like how we get oranges from Florida and oil from Texas at home?" A crease formed on Gina's brow as she tried to understand.

"Pretty much. Imagine if Texas became its own country. Texas could then sell oil to the United States for very high prices. Or

Texas could choose not to sell to the U.S. and sell to some other country that needs it for even higher prices. It would be a serious situation indeed," Gene replied.

"Why does everything have to be about money? Why can't people just help each other out?" Gina wondered out loud.

"Tim, do you want to take that one?" Gene smiled.

"No, sir!" answered Tim with a laugh. "It would take all night. And I don't even know if I have good answer."

"With each step toward independence and more power, products from the countries who want to leave Russia become frighteningly expensive, or not available at all," Gene explained further.

"Well, why do the other countries want to leave Russia anyway? Why do they want to have their own power?" Gina asked.

"Tim, how about this one?" Gene smiled.

"Gina, I can only say that I was born in Georgia. No, not Georgia in U.S. Georgia here. It is small country. George Balanchine was also born there. It is my real home. I do not think of myself as Russian, or part of a large union. I want my country to not be with Russia, because Russia only takes from Georgia. It is too poor to live in my hometown. That is why I am here in Leningrad. To work."

"Tim, I am glad you are here. I am trying to understand all of this. People at the party talked about how Leningrad will again be called St. Petersburg. When was it called St. Petersburg?"

"Your turn, Gene," Tim smiled.

"At one time, St. Petersburg was named after the great tsar, or king, of Russia, Peter the Great. Then came the revolution against the tsars, or kings, and the royalty. The city was then named Leningrad for Nikolai Lenin, a leader of the revolution."

"So, they want to have a tsar again?"

Tim and Gene said together, " We can't answer that."

"Too complicated, right? Okay I give up, too. Tim, please put on some music."

Tim put a New Kids on the Block tape in for her. Gina was glad that her uncle and Tim were there. The political talk had upset her. Everyone was so angry. She loved Tina and her family. She didn't want anything happen to them. After Tim dropped them off, Gina was silent as they climbed the stairs to their own apartment.

"What are you thinking?" her uncle asked.

"I'm worried about the Mikhailovs and Tim's family. I want them to be safe and happy. What's going to happen, Uncle Gene?"

"I am not sure, Gina. We shall have to wait and see. I fear for our friends as well. I cannot say that I do not. We shall work and pray for them. Will we not?"

"Yes, we will. Good night," said Gina as she passed him in the hallway. She went into her room.

"Good night, Gina," she heard Gene say as she turned out her light.

Even though Russia was in trouble, Lily was happy. "I raised a daughter who cares about other people. Gina loves her friends and wants the best for them. She doesn't think only about herself. She cares about the world and how we all live together in it. My little artist will use her dancing to tell others about the world!"

Chapter Fourteen

In spite of the fight at Ilya Alexandrovich's birthday party, it was calming to be with Tina and her grandmother out in the country. One unusually warm Saturday afternoon the girls returned. They liked to gather flowers. Gina pressed them in her uncle's books. After a long hike in the woods, the girls lay back on a blanket looking up at the sky.

Gina told Tina about how her mother used to dance. "She was like you, Tina. She was small and beautiful and emotional. People stopped and looked when she moved or danced. She was part of the music. That was the only time she was happy."

"Why was she not happy when she was not dancing? She danced. What else does one need?" asked Tina.

"She said she felt lonely, and different, except when she was dancing. When my mother danced in the theater she became everyone in the audience, and her role, all at once. People told her after that they loved watching her because she made them feel great," replied Gina.

"That is how artists feel. It is not strange. We are different. We look at world in other way. I want your mother to know she is good and fine," said Tina. Both girls smiled up at the clouds to tell Lily they thought she was the greatest.

Gina thought of the dancers who had graduated from the academy, Mikhail Baryshnikov, Natalya Makarova, and the famous director of the New York City Ballet, George Balanchine.

"Tina, if my mother had studied at the academy, she would have been a great ballerina. She would have been a great choreographer, too."

Tina nodded. "I think she would have been great choreographer. I like to choreograph, too. Maybe you should try, Gina!"

"Maybe someday. Not now. I'm still figuring out how to dance. My mom was inventive. She was always looking out for what was new. Why, my mother would have turned the academy inside out!" decided Gina.

"Yes, she would have been like famous instructor, Agrippina Voganova. She developed ballet method we study. She saw new ideas from young choreographers. She changed method of teaching ballet so dancers could be strong to dance new choreography. She changed ballet forever." Tina made balletic movements with her arms that looked delicate, but that required a lot of muscle.

Gina thought for a moment. She asked, "How come I don't feel like mom did? Don't I look at the world like an artist?"

Tina rolled over onto her stomach. "I don't know how you look at world, Gina. I am not your eyes! Only, you think about self too much to look at world. Artist must show others how to feel and what to feel. It is our work!"

"But can't people just feel on their own? Why do they need us? Why would anyone want to feel like I do?!" asked Gina.

"It is simple. People forget how to feel. We work so they can remember," answered Tina.

"Feeling is so awful and takes up so much time. Aren't people better off skipping the whole thing?" frowned Gina. Tina laughed and threw the gathered flowers at Gina. "I think you are not yet Russian! Come, let's go for tea!" And they ran into the house for thin Russian pancakes called blini with raspberry jam and tea.

The girls walked back to the train station later in the afternoon. They said little on the return trip. The fresh air had tired them. Gina returned to the apartment in the early evening. She found her uncle in the living room examining one of his books.

"Gina, what are these moldy, old flower petals doing in my book?" Gene asked. He pointed out to her pages that had become stained.

"I'm pressing them to save them, Uncle Gene, to remember Russia by. You can still read the words through the spots," Gina replied.

"But, dear Gina, besides ruining my books, it is illegal to take plant material out of the country," he said taking the book from her hand.

"What customs official is going to look in a twelve year-old's bags for pressed flowers?" she logically asked.

"Well, perhaps not. It is the principle of the thing," he said replacing the book on the shelf.

Gina sighed. She took the flowers from him and left the room. She decided to continue to press flowers in the books he never read. "Volume two of *War and Peace* in the original Russian oughta do the trick," Gina thought. She plucked it off the shelf. She placed carefully gathered water violets somewhere in chapter twenty-six. "Can't imagine he'll find these until he's way into retirement," she smiled to herself.

Chapter Fifteen

Gene and Gina's telephone jangled like a teakettle ready to burst with steam. Gene had set it on the softest ring. It didn't matter. Telephones in Russia rang very loudly. Each of their friends had several telephones in their tiny apartments. All were set to ring with the volume at top intensity.

Several times at dinner in the apartments of Gene's colleagues, telephones rang to startle him. Gina had politely looked down to hide her mirth as he leapt from his seat, knocking silverware, glasses, and napkins to the floor. Gina noticed with interest that after exactly three times Gene trained himself to calmly ignore the ring of the telephone.

Today Gina heard the ring of the phone in their apartment. She brushed Sugarplum away from the dial. Gina loved it when the telephone rang. It was better when it was Tina calling her to come over to the Mikhailovs' apartment. It was the best when the phone actually worked. Half the time when she answered, Gina heard nothing on the other end. Then Tina would run down six flights of stairs and out in to the courtyard. She would yell up to Gina in hopes that a window was open in the Shosteks' apartment to, "Come over!"

Gina put the receiver to her ear and listened to Tina say, "Gina, you must come over now! Nick has made new invention!"

Gina answered in delight, "Hey, I can hear you! The phone works!"

"Great! Come over!" Gina heard Tina hang up her phone.

Gina hugged Sugarplum "Good-bye." She raced down five flights of stairs to the courtyard. She raced up another six flights of stairs to the Mikhailovs' apartment. She muttered all the way. "Why couldn't Nick have invented a dumb elevator for heaven's sake, if he's supposed to be such a genius?" She flung open the door to the foyer of the Mikhailov apartment.

Gina was smacked in the forehead by one of Nick's previous inventions. Gina knew it was there. Usually she avoided it. In her haste she had forgotten to bypass the Automatic Hat Receiver. It hung from the ceiling. It was meant to hang the hats of visitors by snatching them off of people's heads. Gina whapped the device away with her hand. She entered the living room cursing.

Tina came to the door as Gina entered, "Sorry about that."

"He's still perfecting it," they groaned together.

Nick never could get the distance from the ceiling to the top of anyone's head right. And he had not ever taken it down from the foyer. He claimed he was still perfecting it. So, it whacked newcomers in the face or about the shoulders, depending on their height. Those who knew the Mikhailovs had long since learned to sidestep the contraption as they came through the door. They clutched their hats near their stomachs in fear of losing them forever.

Gina looked down and petted Sugarplum's brother, Romeo. He had come to greet her. Gina relaxed and smiled. "I love coming to your house, Tina."

"Come sit. I love when you are here." Tina gestured for her to come into the living room.

The Mikailov's home was filled with sound and movement of a delicate nature. Beautiful music might be floating out of any room. Pieces of Tina's fluffy costumes and hair bows made their way into all corners of the apartment. Pink shoe ribbons, tufts of the lamb's wool that she tucked into the toes of her shoes, and the shoes themselves, were strewn across the floor. Little Romeo had been playing with them.

Tables and chairs and sofas were covered with music sheets and choreography notes. They were notes for ballets that Ilya Alexandrovich was working on, or music written by composers that he was using in his work. The rest of the surfaces, tops of bookcases, the refrigerator, the counter tops in the kitchen, were covered with tissue paper diagrams for Nick's inventions. One slightly open window could cause the whole place to flutter like a sea of moths.

The only objects holding anything down were English grammar books and volumes of literature by American and British authors.

Tatiana Ivanovna, Tina's mother, used those books to teach her courses in English Literature at Leningrad State University.

Tina was excited. "Nick has created invention for you, Gina! He is working on it. We must give him little time."

Gina smiled. "A new invention! Tina, why are all of Nick's inventions here and not at his house?"

"Nick spends much time with my parents. They are his uncle and aunt. Nick's father, Anton, is not able to take care of Nick. Sometimes Nick stays with his father. He tries to love his father as he is. It is very difficult." Tina looked serious and sad.

Gina slowly nodded. "I sort of understand. Anyway, show me Nick's inventions. I didn't really look the other times I was here."

Tina picked up some tiny woolen knit items from the floor. "You know, all Nick's inventions sound good. Here are mittens for cat. So mama does not have to dust slippery wooden floors. He put them on Romeo. Gina, Romeo skidded across floor and smashed into wall! Romeo only tried to catch ribbon or spider! I told Nick to invent crash helmet for Romeo, or Feline Dusting Device must go!"

They moved into the kitchen. "What are these, Moon Boots?" Gina picked up a boot with an enormous wedge heel.

"Those are Time-Saving Vegetable Choppers. Nick made mama pair of shoes. Look, you take boxes off bottoms. You put whole vegetables into boxes. On lids of boxes are rows of knives that chop cabbage, carrots, or beets. You only have to wear shoes. You walk in house doing other things. Knives chop vegetables into tiny pieces. Poor mama put cabbages in each shoe and put shoes on. She fell. She wrenched ankle running for ringing telephone!"

"Tina, I'm sorry to laugh, but that's so funny!" Gina put the shoe back on the kitchen floor.

"We laugh, too. Mama made Nick clean up all shreds of cabbage that flew in room. He even found one hanging from edge of picture frame in bedroom. It was far away from where she fell!" Tina led her to Ilya Alexandrovich's study.

"These clocks are pretty," remarked Gina.

"Nick put special sounds for each person on clocks. Mine has *Dance of Sugarplum Fairy*. I hear and I go to ballet lesson." The girls listened to the light, tinkly music. They danced around the room.

"What sound does your mom have?" Gina picked up a clock with an English bulldog's face painted on it.

"It has Winston Churchill's voice saying, 'This is England's finest hour.' Then mama knows to go to university. She loves English writers."

Gina turned on the alarm for Ilya Alexandrovich. She laughed. It was French can-can music.

Tina giggled, too. "That is when papa goes to academy. And Nick, the inventor, never goes to school without hearing this." The Metro-Goldwyn-Mayer lion roared.

Gina smiled. "These are great! But all of you are always late for everything."

"Russian clocks never work, Gina." Tina set the lion clock down and led her back to the living room.

"Then why do people buy them?" Gina put down the French can-can clock and followed Tina.

"They work for while and then stop," Tina answered.

"That's why there are so many clock repair shops! There's one on almost every street! These clocks work. Why are you always late?" Gina looked at family photos on the wall as she followed Tina down the hallway.

Tina pointed her nose in the air. "I not always late. Well, maybe most times. Anyway, alarms go off, but not when we ask them to go off. One night alarm went off at four in morning! I was afraid I was late! I put on clothes, brushed teeth, and grabbed dance bag. I looked out. I saw it was night. I went to Nick's bedroom. I hit Mr. Inventor with pointe shoe right in nose!"

The girls laughed and Nick entered the room. He rolled out a table. It bore an object covered in cloth. Gina wondered what the invention would be. Gina and Tina sat on the sofa patiently waiting for him to reveal his surprise. Gina hoped the invention had nothing to do with grabbing stuff off of people. Her forehead still hurt from the hat thing.

Nick triumphantly tore off the cloth. He revealed a radio. Nick declared, "Gina, I made short wave. You may listen to Minneapolis!" He turned it on. She could faintly hear the local news and weather from her old hometown.

Gina jumped up. "Nick, this is great! I can listen to my own music!"

They tuned it to the KDWB station. "It's Vanilla Ice!" They all sang along to *Play That Funky Music.*

"Sometime you can hear Minnesota Twins play baseball!" said Nick.

Gina picked up the radio and gently held it in her arms. "Nick, thank you for doing this for me and my uncle. It is a wonderful invention. And a wonderful present."

Nick looked down and blushed when he saw Gina's joy at his creation. Tina noticed it. Gina did, too.

Chapter Sixteen

Gina was terrified that she would forget the details of her mother. She missed Lily terribly. Sugarplum helped. Gina was thankful to Tina for her. When things became too much, Gina ran past Valerya Isidorovna into her room. She scooped Sugarplum up into her arms. She told the kitten everything she could remember about her mother.

Each day that passed Gina stared into a photograph of her mother. She tried to remember how it felt to be with her. The picture was from Gina's first day of kindergarten. Mother and daughter smiled at their elderly neighbor, Mrs. Wheat, who had come by to take a photo of the special occasion.

Before kindergarten Gina remembered being happiest watching cartoons, drawing, and dancing by herself. On Gina's first day of kindergarten, Lily dressed her in a pretty pale blue dress. She set her on the couch until it was time to leave. Gina's father was out of town somewhere. Gina stood up, walked to the bathroom, and was sick. Lily came rushing in, "Gina, are you okay? What can I do? Are you nervous about school?"

"No, I'm fine," Gina calmly answered.

"Do you have a fever?" Lily touched her forehead. "You don't feel warm."

"Let's go, mom!" Gina was too little to be able to tell her mother how terrified she was. She wanted to go to school and get the day over with. She was afraid the other kids wouldn't like her. She walked with Lily to school. Lily reluctantly left her there.

Later when Lily arrived to walk her home, Gina danced happily up to her. "Mom, we got to paint at real easels! And we learned a chicken dance!"

"Honey, that's wonderful!" Both had forgotten about the morning's incident. Gina remembered Lily smiling glowingly at her, but that was all. She couldn't recall anything else from that day.

Gina rearranged Sugarplum in her arms and looked at the photograph again. She tried to pretend that the picture of her mother smiling into the camera, was Lily smiling at her now in her bedroom. Out of the photograph, Lily smiled at Gina with the deepest depths of her soul and the fiercest force of her love. Gina basked in Lily's charming smile. She continued to pet Sugarplum.

"Gina, Valerya Isidorovna has dinner ready!" called Gene.

Gina set Sugarplum on her bed. "I'm coming, Uncle Gene." She left her bedroom.

"Oh, Gina," Lily thought. "I know you felt abandoned and lonely. I tried to protect you from pain. I watched as you read books and painted pictures and danced. I know you tried fill yourself up with a father's love that wasn't there. I love you so much!"

The following day at the academy she had a private lesson with Ilya Alexandrovich. He had decided that once a week Gina should have a private lesson with him on top of her other ballet classes. Progress was slow. Ilya Alexandrovich sat on a wooden chair as he watched Gina perfom a slow, balancing adagio for him in the center of the studio.

When she was finished he asked, "Gina, why did you choose to dance ballet? Why not jazz or modern?"

"I don't know. Because my mother gave me ballet slippers and not tap shoes," said Gina.

"Are you sure that is only reason?" he pressed. "Of course it's the only reason, I was six years old! How would I know what I wanted to do?" Gina shot back. She sighed and politely asked, "Ilya Alexandrovich, why did you choose ballet?"

He sat back in his chair and folded his arms across his chest. "Because my dear, I am here to tell stories. Ballet does so. Modern dance and jazz give depth and color. Tap dancing leads minds to Broadway fantasy and dreamland. Only ballet tells us joys, sorrows, heartfelt longings, and simple everyday feelings of common soul. Lavish, beautiful costumes proclaim victory and success. But it is feet and pointe shoes, my dear, that tell how and what soul feels. Task is large. You will meet challenge well."

Gina sighed again. She walked to the center of the room to try the steps again. She dimly thought, "I could have been given jazz shoes and been saddled with giving color. But, no, I had to get silly ballet slippers. I have to tell the whole darn story of humanity!"

Gina finished the lesson in a bad mood. "You must try more. You must not be scared," Ilya Alexandrovich said as she curtsied to him. Gina left thinking, "Well, I am scared and I am trying!"

Tim's music could not cheer her on the way home. At home Gina had an annoying conversation with her uncle.

"Gina, your books and clothes are strewn from one end of the apartment to the other. If it is at all possible, might you please stow them in your room?" Gene asked with irritation from the sofa where he read the paper.

"Uncle Gene, I hardly fit in my room. I've noticed that a lion's share of the apartment is devoted to your things. Valerya Isidorovna moves everything anyway. I can't find anything anywhere. Except for those dumb slippers. I hate slippers. I refuse to wear them. I don't care if it is the national custom."

Gina paced back and forth in front of the coffee table. "And I refuse to put on all of my outdoor clothes in the apartment and then sweat to death walking down five flights to the street. She makes me wear a scarf. It's thirty degrees outside! Even Grandma Shostek wouldn't make me do that! They itch! She's a nice lady and everything. I know she cooks and all that, but she drives me crazy!"

Gina stopped and looked at Gene. "And can't I please, please, go out alone in the city a little more often?" Gina realized Gene would never consider that. She decided to give in on that particular point. She added, "At least out alone with Tina?"

Gene turned his paper to a new page. "Oh, all right. No more slippers, but in the homes of our friends you must put on slippers when you enter the house as they are presented to you. You are released from wearing scarves, unless I say it is cold enough to wear one."

"Big deal," thought Gina. Then she pleaded, "I know it's okay to go alone out to the country to visit Tina's grandma, but can't we go out around here more often? We're only three blocks from Nevsky

Avenue. I promise to go out only when it's still light out. Plus, we'll get more exercise if Tim doesn't have to drive us around all the time." She waited breathlessly for the granting of her final wish.

Gene frowned slightly. He said, "You get plenty of exercise. But, only because of your mother's desire that you learn to be independent, I will allow going out alone with Tina. Only if I and Tina's parents know where you will be. And only if we know exactly when you are to return. I will notify Valerya Isidorovna that you are to be allowed to go out in the city more often with Tina. I will talk with her about the slippers and the other things."

"Good thing. She'd never believe me if I told her," remarked Gina.

"Gina, I expect you to treat Valerya Isidorovna with respect," cautioned Gene.

"I do, Uncle Gene. It's not that. I call her by that big, long name and everything. And I won't let her carry heavy bags. She doesn't listen to me like she does to you. She yells at me what to do all the time. Well, not yells, but, she's on me all the time! Do this! Do that! I thought she'd just do her stuff and then tell me about the old days, like other grandmothers do," explained Gina.

"I understand now, Gina. I will talk to her about listening to you. The situation you are describing is a result of our cultural differences. She cares very much about you. I will explain that by listening to you, she will let you know that she cares about you. And what's more, that you are interested in her life," Gene said.

"Hey, thanks," said Gina as she hugged him. She did like Gene. He could be such a good guy.

Gene spoke with Valerya Isidorovna. Gina listened from the next room. She picked out some of the Russian words. Gina heard something about her getting sick without slippers, scarves, and bundling up in thick clothing. She was pretty sure Valerya Isidorovna said that Gina would get lost in the city. Gene said something about Tina being with her. Valerya Isidorovna threw up her hands. She finally said, "Noo, ladnah." That meant "Okay." Gina was free! She slept more easily that night.

Spring wore on. The weather became warmer. Leningraders came out in force into the crowded streets. Gina and Tina found themselves sandwiched on busses, trams, trolleybuses, and the metro, even when it wasn't rush hour. Fearing that her ribs would break, she refused to ride them. Gina said she would become physically ill if she did.

The girls went most places on foot. The stores and movie theaters were crowded. People walked five abreast on the sidewalk. People walked too close for Gina, who had been raised in a three-bedroom house with a generous yard.

One afternoon after school the girls were struggling to walk along the crowded sidewalk. Gina had an idea. She grabbed Tina's arm. She said, "We must go to the ballet academy right now! And I mean now!"

Tina said, "Gina, Gina, okay, okay, we go there!" Gina entered the largest rehearsal hall at the academy. She stood dead center in it.

"I do not understand why you do this, Gina," commented Tina. She sat on the bench of the grande piano in one corner of the hall.

Gina breathed, "Because if I stand exactly in the center of this large place, I am as far away from another human being as I can possibly be in Leningrad."

"And it matters not to you that here have danced not only Anna Pavlova, but Vaslav Nijinsky, Rudolph Nureyev, and Mikhail Baryshnikov?" reminded Tina.

"Not a bit. If any of them try to get near me I'll scream," exclaimed Gina.

Back out on the street in the crowds, Tina suggested that the girls take a trolleybus the few short blocks to Rubinstein Street. She felt cold.

"Cold! Tina, this is spring! Minnesota is like Siberia. It gets to thirty-degrees-below wind chill! This is nothing. It must be forty degrees outside! No! No more jam-packed buses. No more grandmothers telling me what to do all the time!" Tina tried to hold down Gina's flailing arms and hands as waved them excitedly. People were beginning to stare.

"No, Tina! No more standing in stupid lines that go nowhere! No, I will not wait in line in a store for one person to tell me how much something costs. And then go to another line to a second person to wait to pay for it. And then to a third line and a third person to pick up what I want to buy! No! No! No! Why do you do things this way? It's dumb and a waste of time!" Gina ranted.

Tina gave her a little smile and replied, "We like to keep busy." Both of them laughed. Tina let go of Gina's arms.

Gina wasn't angry anymore. "You know what? I figured out why my Uncle Gene gets along so well in the city. He doesn't have to do anything by himself! Tim drives him everywhere. Valerya Isidorovna does everything with the apartment, laundry, or shopping. All of his work stuff is handled for him at the consulate. He probably doesn't even know that half the time the telephone doesn't work! You and I are practically having a friendship via ESP!"

"Gina, I have seen Gene use phone in apartment. He knows that sometimes it not work. And you asked that you and I be allowed to go in city alone without Tim, remember?"

"Well, it's just that Uncle Gene brags about knowing Leningrad so well from the old days when he was in college."

"Gina, now I am warm from arguing. We can walk home and not take trolleybus." They started for home.

"So much for the great Dr. Shostek having a real Russian experience," Gina fumed. "I bet he's never even been on the subway!"

"Gina, you are silly girl. Gene went on subway in old university days! Come, let's race!" Tina started running with Gina close behind. They both ran laughing to Rubinstein Street. They dodged and weaved between other people on the street as much as they could.

Chapter Seventeen

A few evenings later, Gina smiled at her uncle at dinner. "Uncle Gene, I don't see you any more. You're gone when I get up in the morning. Valerya Isidorovna stays later and later every night until you get home. Is everything okay? Did you meet a girl?"

Gene stabbed a pickled mushroom with his fork. "Things have been extremely difficult at the consulate. The people are turning against President Gorbachev. I am frightened of what might happen to him"

Gina stopped eating. "Mom told me about President Kennedy being assassinated. We learned about Abraham Lincoln in school. Is somebody going to kill President Gorbachev?"

"Gina, I hope not. Last October at a national holiday celebration, there was a man in the crowd. President Gorbachev was speaking. The man had a machine gun. Russian Secret Service agents found him before anything happened. The man was arrested and taken away."

"So, what's going on? I don't really know what you do at the consulate." Gina took a bite of cucumber salad.

Gene leaned back in his chair and gestured with his hands as he talked. "It is probably best that you do not know. There are whispers of change, of great, terrifying change in Russia. The people are restless and angry. No one knows if President Gorbachev will stay in power. Someone may try to take his place."

"When will all of this change happen, Uncle Gene?" Sugarplum jumped up into Gina's lap and she stroked her back.

Gene put down his napkin and got up from the table. "I cannot explain just now."

"I know, I know. It's too complicated. I'm going to do my homework." Gina stood up, still holding Sugarplum, and started down the hallway to her room.

"Good night, Gina. I will be working at the consulate long after you are asleep. Valerya Isidorovna will stay here until I return."

"Well, I'm tired. I'll probably go to bed."

Gina pretended to sleep. She heard Gene getting ready to go out. She started down the long, narrow hall of their apartment. Valerya Isidorovna was in the living room. Gina peeked into Gene's bedroom. He was dressed in a dark wool coat, baggy dark pants, and a stretchy, woolen cap.

"Wow, Uncle Gene, you look like you're going to go steal diamonds or something," said Gina. She rounded the corner into his room. He started. She said, "I know, I know, I should be in bed."

"You should. I have not told you about this. In case you are ever questioned, I do not want you to feel the need to lie," he said. He turned and adjusted his cap in the mirror. "You make a great spy! Mom would love this! She always said you were so boring!" Gina exclaimed. She leaned against the bedroom door.

He turned to Gina. "Boring! What? Oh, never mind. I am not spying!

Gina leaned farther into the room "What are you dressed as anyway?"

"A Russian worker. What do you think I look like?" He frowned.

"Like I said, a diamond thief from a movie. You look too neat, Uncle Gene. Untuck your shirt. Mess up your hair a little." He did as he was told.

She looked at him head to toe. "Better. Where are you going?"

"I attend political meetings that are now freely open to the public. I gather information there. It is important that they believe that I am a Russian," Gene defended himself.

"I bet you don't tell 'em that you go back to the consulate and spill your guts about everything you hear!" challenged Gina.

Gene buttoned is coat. "Often I do not get that far. Sometimes doors are closed in my face as I try to slip into political meetings. My accent gives me away. They do not trust that I am from their neighborhood."

"Well, they're right. You're not from their neighborhood. But your Russian is great. How can they tell?" Gina jumped up to mess his hair a little more.

"The spy novels of my youth were right. A Russian can always tell when a person is not born speaking Russian. In Russian spy novels that is how spies are discovered. If I say one word incorrectly, it is all over for me. If anyone finds out that I am reporting everything back to the U.S. consulate I will be thrown out of town." Gene put on dark leather gloves.

"I don't want us to be thrown out of town! Leather gloves, Uncle Gene, really? That will give you away for sure."

He reconsidered and took off the gloves. "I do not think that I will be discovered tonight. Often, I slip in unnoticed. I go into the meetings. I make friendly comments to the Russians. Then I eavesdrop. I cover up my silence with a hacking cough. It is easier to go undetected if I do not speak to anyone."

"I think you're enjoying this, Uncle Gene. Maybe you'll meet a girl!" Gina took the gloves from him and placed them on the dresser.

"Stop going on about that! I never should have told you a thing about this. I consider it research. Now, Gina, return to your bed!" said her uncle. He gently shoved her back down the hall toward her room.

Gina worried about him. She could not sleep until he was safely home. "Just when I was starting to have some peace around here. This could stunt my growth!" she thought. She pounded the pillow and turned over. She listened for her uncle to return.

He did finally. She awakened to hear him say "Good Night" to Valerya Isidorovna. Then she heard Tim's car pull away. Still she didn't sleep well.

The following day at lessons with Ilya Alexandrovich, Gina performed a solo he had choreographed for her. She finished. He softly said, "Gina you must push harder. You must go beyond what you know." She danced the solo again.

He was sitting in his usual wooden chair on front of the mirror. "Gina, you must show more. Show more of self!"

Gina argued. "But, this is me, Ilya Alexandrovich! There isn't any more of me to show!"

"Again!" He commanded. She danced the solo again the same way she had the first two times.

Ilya Alexandrovich raised his voice. "Gina, you must work harder. I must see joy and passion! Is not enough!"

Gina rudely replied. "You mean I'm not enough!"

"Gina, do not twist words. Solo. Again." Ilya Alexandrovich pointed to the center of the studio. Gina danced again. She dramatically pretended she felt joy and passion.

"Gina! I do not want fake! Must be real!" he shouted.

She stamped her foot in exasperation. "You're trying to get me to be something I'm not, Ilya Alexandrovich! I can't do what you want. I'm not like Tina!"

Ilya Alexandrovich was standing. He waved his hands wildly. "I cannot work so! You must believe in self! How much longer you going to wait! Leave fear and go on! Make mistake! Try! Fall down! Get up, but try!"

"Fine, I'll leave. You won't have to bother with me anymore," she said. She turned and left the room.

Lily looked down at them from the ceiling. She sighed. Then she looked around the studio. "At last, I am at the Kirov School! I simply can't stay in the apartment anymore!" she thought. "I feel for you, Gina. I know how hard you are trying. Trying to be the perfect niece, student, friend, and ballerina. "Oh, Gina," Lily softly whispered, "You are holding inside so many frightening things. Please let Ilya Alexandrovich help you."

Gina returned to the studio.

Lily smiled down at her daughter.

Gina stood uncertainly at the door. "Ilya Alexandrovich, may I come in?"

He was still standing in the middle of the studio where she had left him. "You may, Gina."

She solemnly curtsied twice to him. "I am sorry that I was rude to you. It was disrespectful of me to leave the studio. I was angry and frustrated. It's not your fault I can't dance."

"Gina, my dear. You are lovely dancer. I train you to be professional. I must always ask for more than you give. And sometimes I must be harsh." He nodded solemnly.

She looked seriously into his eyes. "You can threaten all you like. It just didn't seem to help me."

"I see future dancer you will be. You cannot see as I do. I push you to become ballerina I see you becoming." The old man brushed the hair off of Gina's forehead. He put his arm around her shoulder, as he would have to Tina.

He left her and sat down in his chair. "And now, we begin again."

Gina went to the center of the room. She stood in fifth position with arms in preparation. She waited for the music to begin.

Lily was happy to see she had taught Gina some things well before she had to leave her.

That evening as she got ready for bed, Gina looked at her calendar. She counted the days until her recital. The recital was set for the beginning of June. Time was running out, Gina thought. She wasn't any closer to having courage.

She thought over and over about what Ilya Alexandrovich told her. The part about telling a story with her dancing. Could she make up stories? Telling a story with her dancing. But, what story could she tell? She felt sure that Ilya Alexandrovich wasn't interested in silly stories.

She and Lily had made up silly stories together every night before bed. Those were the only stories that she had ever made up. Besides, Lily had helped her.

There it was, another thing in her life to remind her that her mother was gone. Staring at the purple and blue pansy wallpaper, she slipped into sleep cursing Ilya Alexandrovich and his idiotic teaching methods.

Chapter Eighteen

The girls were allowed to see a matinee performance of the ballet *Scheherazade*. They were taking the tram to the theater. It was not rush hour and a Sunday. Gina felt comfortable getting on the nearly empty tram. She had never been on one before. People did not ride trams as often because they traveled so slowly. Often the wires on the roof of the tram became disconnected from the electric lines above and they stopped dead on the tracks.

Tina showed Gina how to put a ten-kopeck coin into the moneybox. Then she tore a ticket off of a roll showing that she had paid to ride. The ticket could just as easily be ripped off of the roll without a deposit of the kopecks.

"Why do people bother to pay? They could just rip off a ticket and ride for free," said Gina.

"Because they are honest. Everyone on the tram would see them if they sat down with not paying." The girls found two seats together.

"What do they do with the ticket? Does someone collect them?" Gina slid in to the seat next to the window.

"No."Tina sat down in the aisle seat.

"Tina, that's silly. Then why do they have to have a ticket?"

"Because sometimes official people come onto the tram to check to see if people have tickets." Tina smiled at a baby in his mother's arms across the aisle from them.

"Tickets that they could take without paying for anyway?!" Gina asked. She thought to herself, "How stupid."

"Gina, it is best not to try to understand some things," said Tina.

The ballet was at the Kirov Theater of Opera and Ballet. The theater had been called The Mariinsky Theater before Russia's revolution. After the revolution the new leader, Nikolai Lenin, renamed it for one of his friends. The theater was over two hundred years old. It was the home of the Kirov Opera and Ballet companies. The girls got off of the tram. Gina saw that the theater was a beautiful, light blue color.

They entered the building, crossed the marble floor over to an usher, and showed their tickets. The girls floated up several marble staircases. Gina looked up into the high arches that formed the ceiling in the lobby of the theater. All was white and gold with many dazzling chandeliers.

They gave their coats to the woman in coat check. They rented opera glasses.

Gina asked,"What if I wanted to keep my coat in case I got cold?"

"You cannot. It is not allowed," replied Tina.

Coat check was another Russian thing that seemed stupid to Gina. Elderly women raced back and forth as crowds of people arriving for the matinee swelled to check their coats. The people waited for them to be hung up and be given a token to reclaim the coat later. How much simpler it would be, Gina thought, if everyone draped their coats across the back of their seat.

Gina adjusted the waistband of her black skirt. It was covered with small, red flowers. She loved how the skirt felt as it swirled around her ankles. But she hated how the waistband rode around her waist as she walked. This left her twisted up in the skirt until she unwound herself. Tina wore a plain, pale blue dress that fell straight from her shoulders to right below her knees. It floated around her as she walked.

On the way to their seats Tina greeted several of her classmates from the academy. She introduced Gina to them. They said "Zdrastvooitye," to one of Tina's instructors.

"So many kids go to the ballet?" asked Gina.

Tina answered as she waved to another fellow ballet student, "Yes, it is very popular. Children go to ballet, even who not study ballet."

"Wow, I've only seen crowds this big at football games at home in Minneapolis. The only time the ballet is packed is when they do the *Nutcracker* at Christmas."

"American football! Will you show me how to play? Then I can beat Nick at it!" They continued up the curving staircase.

"Me? No. Maybe Harry could teach you. He works with my uncle. He's always reading the sports pages. My uncle hates it."

Gina looked down at the scooped out places on the stairs. Thousands of pairs of shoes had worn down the marble stairs over the hundreds of years that people had gone to see the ballet at the Kirov Theater.

They reached an inner balcony surrounding a lobby that was used during the intermissions. They saw more glittering chandeliers that had been hung to light the beautiful expansive room. There were white sculptures all around on pedestals. There was a counter where one could buy champagne, compote, little sandwiches, or chocolate. Compote, Gina knew from visiting Tina's grandmother, was fruit juice with bits of real fruit floating inside. It was served in small glasses. Cherry was the best kind. The girls each bought a chocolate bon-bon wrapped in a picture of a ballerina.

They continued on toward their seats. Again Tina showed their tickets. They were led to the private door of a box. They entered and sat in stiff-backed red velvet upholstered chairs.

Gina leaned out of the box and opened her eyes wide. There were five balconies. Each was fancily decorated with swirling patterns and curlicues, cherubs and angels. Gina breathed, "This is so beautiful! Gina settled back into her seat. "Why don't you walk like a duck like the other ballet students? Those girls we met in the lobby looked stuck up and they walked like ducks."

"It is bad for knees and ankles. I don't do. Other girls walk with feet like duck to show off that they attend academy of ballet. Mama bought tickets for us on damskaya side of theater. Do you know this word?" Tina unwrapped her chocolate. She offered Gina half.

"No. What is the damskaya side of the theater?" Gina mumbled with chocolate in her mouth.

"Damskaya side, is side of left in theater. It comes from word for madame. It is stage left to us. To you in English theater, it is stage right. We say what side of stage by facing stage. You say stage side by facing audience. You see?" said Tina licking the last bit of chocolate from her fingers.

"Do I see? Tina, are you kidding? That was in English, and I have no idea what you were talking about! You're starting to sound like my uncle. Never mind, I guess I don't want to know anyway." The two giggled.

The girl's box was on the first level. Tina explained that it was one level below the level where the tsar, or king, used to sit. Tina pointed across the theater. "Moozhskaya is other side. It comes from word for husband."

"Husband? What is the word for husband?" asked Gina.

"It is moozh," whispered Tina. The last of the bells rang, calling people to their seats.

"Moozh, what a funny word," thought Gina. The house lights darkened and the conductor appeared in the orchestra pit. Everyone applauded and the overture began.

The curtain had yet to go up. Gina watched the orchestra. The violinists sat in perfect order, concertmaster, first chair violin, then second chair, and so on. The curves of their bodies moved together. Each violin bow tilted at exactly the same angle and in complete unison. Gina was delighted to hear a lovely violin solo in the overture. She had listened to it on a stereo at home. Now she heard it lusciously played in the theater.

"That Rimsky-Korsakov sure knew what he was doing when he wrote this," sighed Gina. Her eyes wandered over and over again to the second chair violin. Gina watched him carefully. His bow fairly bounced off the strings. "Show off," she thought. The concertmaster, who had all of the solos, did not do that. His bow calmly rested a quarter of an inch from the strings after each time he played.

None of that mattered, especially. What mattered was that the second chair violin was dark-haired and dark-eyed. He wore a tuxedo. He was the handsomest man Gina had ever seen. She tore open her program. The name of the second chair violin was so beautiful she could hardly stand it.

"Maximillien Dmitrievich Lozanov, perfect," she sighed. The curtain rose. The ballerinas came on and off stage in their colorful tutus and danced a million steps. Gina did not notice them.

Gina left the Kirov Theater wordlessly. Her mouth was set. She tried hard to keep her new, delicious secret. Should she tell Tina?

"Why can't I be someone else?" Gina thought. "Someone older and more beautiful. Someone who always knows the right thing to say. What would Gabriela do in a spot like this?" Gina wondered to herself.

Gabriela was a fictitious ballerina that Lily and Gina had created. Gabriela was always in a delightfully pleasant mood. She dressed beautifully and was adored by all. Fans, the press, and cameras followed Gabriela everywhere she went. Lily told Gina many bedtime stories about Gabriela having fascinating adventures all over the world.

Gina thought, "If Gabriela were meeting Maximillien she would wear something long and sweeping. She would chat about interesting things. Gabriela would tell Maximillien about the solos she was preparing to dance at places like the Paris Opera Ballet or Covent Garden."

Gina's mind pictured a scene in an elegantly furnished dressing room. Gina, imagining she was Gabriela, entered her dressing room. Gina/Gabriela had danced beautifully in *Swan Lake*. She had been given a standing ovation. Gina/Gabriela changed into a gown of scarlet red. Diamonds glittered in her ears and at her throat.

A dark-eyed gentleman in a tuxedo was ushered into her dressing room. Her hand flew to her mouth in surprise. He had watched her dance, enraptured, from the middle of the first row of the theater. He apologized for being so forward as to come to introduce himself. She had danced so exquisitely, he couldn't resist. She would call him "Max," of course...

On the tram on the way home Tina chattered about the prima ballerina and how beautifully she had danced. Gina did not hear her. Tina finally noticed that Gina wasn't listening to her. They were on the tram riding back home. Gina gazed about as though she was breathing the scent of exotic flowers.

"You not watch ballet!" Tina accused her. "You only watch orchestra."

"I was watching how well the musicians followed the dancers. Do you know anything about the second chair violin?" Gina asked in what she hoped was a casual voice. She didn't want to give away her passionate interest in Maximillien Dmitrievich Lozanov.

"Yes, sure, that is Max. He is friend of papa's. He is composer. He only plays in orchestra at ballet to live. He wishes only to write music. I can arrange meeting. He is nice man," said Tina.

They got off at their stop and skipped across the street to the ice-cream kiosk. Luckily, Gina liked vanilla. It was the only flavor they ever sold. And it was the best icecream she had ever had.

"What about our Nick?" Tina asked. "He is kind and handsome. He likes you very well."

"Nick?" Gina murmured. She trailed along behind Tina. Gina wondered about Max. "A composer! And to meet him! But could she ever call him moozh with a straight face?" Tina didn't say anything more about Nick. Gina wouldn't have heard anything she said anyway.

Lily twirled in the air as she floated behind the girls. Lily loved seeing the ballet at the Kirov Theater. Gina and Tina didn't know that Lily had hovered just above and behind them the whole time they were in the theatre. "The dancers were lovely. Scheherazade was beautiful. My Gina, having a crush! Oh, dear!" Lily thought.

Lily tried with all of her might and will to get through to her daughter that afternoon and on into the evening. "Gina is too young to be thinking about someone as old as Max. Gina should have a sweet, innocent friendship with Nick. He is a wonderful young man."

No matter how Lily concentrated her thoughts, she couldn't seem to relay her message to Gina. She looked down from the ceiling at her daughter. Gina slowly brushed her hair and gazed into the mirror. Gina sighed contentedly and climbed into bed. Lily took up her usual perch over Gina's bed.

As Gina was falling asleep, she remembered her mother's stories about boyfriends. One afternoon at home in Minneapolis, Lily had told Gina that she had gone on exactly four dates in high school.

She was invited to the formal proms each spring. The boys sometimes asked Lily five months in advance of the actual dance. Lily admitted to Gina that most boys didn't interest her. Boys were drawn to Lily's beauty, but soon gave up trying to understand her. "I had no interest in saying things most girls said. I felt silly saying the stupid things I heard other girls saying to boys," Lily explained to Gina that afternoon.

Gina knew that as tiny and delicate as Lily was, her mother couldn't pretend to be weak or helpless. Lily sighed that day at their old house, "I was different. No way to fix that. It's no surprise I picked your father. I never did have any luck in love." Gina remembered feeling relieved that her dad left them, even though she didn't understand why he left.

In her bed in Leningrad, Gina pulled her comforter closer to her and felt a twinge of fear. "I can't pretend to be helpless either! What if I'm just like mom? What if I'm different? What if I pick someone like dad? What if Max likes the kind of girls who were mean to me at St. Elizabeth's?" She remembered Max was a friend of Ilya Alexandrovich. He must be nice. She sighed and turned over in her pretty bed.

She had a troubling thought about Nick. She decided not to think about Nick. Besides, she couldn't figure out what it was about him that was bothering her.

Chapter Nineteen

One afternoon Gina found a stack of papers on the dining room table. It was a story that Lily had written. Gene must have found it in some of his things and left it for her to read. She began reading and thought, "This is good!" She settled down in her uncle's easy chair. She let Sugarplum into her lap and continued reading.

The Forest
A Bedtime Story
by Lily Shostek

She had entered a Forest on earth. It was a small Forest, but a Forest nevertheless. All the Animals who lived there did not know that other places existed outside of their Forest. Only this place existed to them. The Animals clamored for attention amongst themselves.

First, she came upon the Alligator. She saw that he had a rough, bumpy skin that covered a wound. The wound was old and deep. A streak of red showed through. It was a hurt that only she could see. The Alligator sensed this and bit at her ankles. He wanted to keep her tenderness far from him and his secret. She stepped away from him. She looked up into the tall Trees that encircled her. She could see sky peeking through the tops of them.

Sometimes a Wind came. It was so strong it nearly bent the Trees double in half backwards. It was a different sort of Wind. It rattled about disrupting what had been set down. But it brought no warmth or gentle rain upon its breezes.

Each morning she arose to clear away the upset that the Wind had wrought the night before. This angered the Wind. He threw stones and leaves and bits of twig at her. She nearly had the Forest in order. The Wind blew through destroying all of her careful labors. In the beginning she laughed. Then he came with force and knocked her over. She was not fast enough to escape him. The other Animals in the Forest widened their eyes and covered their mouths. She was alone. She had no one to smile at, and no one smiled at her. She started to wither.

One day she climbed to the top of the tallest Tree to feel the sun. To her surprise she saw a Man in a Tree not far from her own. They stretched out their hands to one another. The Wind became jealous. He caused the Trees to sway so that they could not touch. The Wind blew so loudly she could not hear the Man's words. Other days she climbed to the treetops to look out and beyond. Sometimes he was in his Tree looking back at her.

She did not know what to call him. No name seemed to fit. She knew his eyes when he let her see what was burning behind them. She tried to imagine a name for him. She cast them aside. Only a name sounding like her name felt right. The Man with Fire in His Eyes was like her somehow. Even when they were apart, they looked up out of the Forest into the sky. They knew that the other was doing the same thing, at the same time.

Someone new came into the Forest. She was a Wild Friend. Wild Friend understood her without words. They made up games together. They set the Forest to right as quickly as they could before the Wind came. When she was tired she put her head on Wild Friend's shoulder. She took Wild Friend to the tops of the Trees to listen to the Man with Fire in His Eyes. With the Wind thrashing as it did, Wild Friend also could not hear him. Soon the Wind took Wild Friend away.

Once more she climbed upward to look for the Man with Fire in his Eyes. At last she heard him. "There are three things that you must do. This is the first. The Wind will destroy you, if you do not stand alone, and strong in his presence. As you do this, you must also uncover the part of you that loves."

Although it frightened her, she learned to cover herself and stand strong. She allowed the Wind to see the precious part of her soul that loved.

Then the Man with Fire in his Eyes told her the second thing. "You must speak your soul and be heard. To do this, you must close yourself to the rumblings and whispers of the Wind and of the Animals in the Forest. "And this is the third thing. You must listen to your own voice as you stand swaying in the Wind with your heart open."

She thought this an odd request coming from a Man who could not be heard over the Wind. She thought that letting everyone see her soul must be enough, but she listened. She did as he said. She did the three things.

She climbed to the top of the tallest Tree. The Animals laughed and chattered. The Alligator snapped at her ankles, but she did not fall. The Wind tried to seduce her with warmth and gentleness. She almost rested, but she knew that she must speak. She straightened her shoulders and leaned into the Wind. He found sand to blind her eyes and to deafen her ears.

She did not fall. She swayed and looked through the sand in her eyes to the treetops and out into the sky. She was afraid. She wildly searched for the Man with Fire in His Eyes across the Trees. She called to him. She was unable to hear her voice over the Wind. She could not find him. She remembered the Fire in his Eyes. She kept him safe within her. She bent her head and was quiet.

She opened her eyes. The Wind was soft. The Alligator had slithered away. She let the sand fall from her eyes and ears. She looked up and saw the treetops parting. The heavens opened themselves up to her. In that moment she saw the part of the Universe that loves. For the first time she heard her own voice. She felt a hand clasping hers. She smiled up at the Man with the Fire in his Eyes. She knew that she now had Fire in her own.

The End

Gene had arrived. He stood in the doorway, watching his niece reading.

Gina looked up. "Uncle Gene, this is fantastic! When did mom write it? What does it mean? It's not at all like the Gabriela stories."

He set down his briefcase. "I do not remember exactly. I believe she wrote it when she was cast in a modern ballet. She wrote the story to act out as she danced the movements. She said that then the movements made sense to her. She was only in high school. Everyone said that she was beautiful in her part, that I do recall. I do confess, I am not entirely sure precisely what the story meant to your mother," Gene replied.

Gina did not tell her uncle about Maximillien Dmitrievich Lozanov. She didn't tell Gene how the story reminded her of Max. Gina went into her room. She sat down on her featherbed. She thought, "Finally, I have a story I can use when I dance! This is what Ilya Alexandrovich means about telling a story with ballet. I only have to think about Max!" She looked at her pointe shoes in the corner of the room. She looked uncertainly at the story in her hand. She wondered if it would work.

That evening she showed the story to Tina. They were in Tina's room sewing ribbons onto their pointe shoes.

"It is wonderful!" exclaimed Tina. "What did beautiful story mean for your mother?"

"I asked Uncle Gene. He's not sure. She probably wouldn't have told him anyway. I mean, he is her brother. She wrote it so she could understand a modern dance she performed."

"Yes, that is good thing to do. Then audience understands better, too. What does story mean for you, Gina?"

Gina told Tina her secret.

"And Max is Man with Fire in Eyes? Gina, that is lovely thought. But, maybe someone... younger, might be nicer for you?" Tina asked.

"Younger? Tina, I don't have a crush on Max or anything, well..."

"You just have crush on him!" Tina said and both girls laughed.

"Who are other creatures in story? Alligator? Other animals?" Tina asked.

"I think the Alligator is how sad I feel about mom dying. The other animals are the snobs at the International School and at St. Elizabeth's. Wild Friend is you and a little of mom mixed together. The Wind is the crazy things that are happening here in Leningrad," answered Gina thoughtfully. "I am part Wild Friend? Thank you, Gina. I am proud! You must let Papa arrange meeting with Man with Fire in Eyes. Max is very nice composer and teacher. He can help you to understand music, like Papa," Tina insisted.

"No, Tina! I can't! I just can't!" Gina cried. On the other hand she thought, just to talk with him a little about music might be nice.

"I'll think about it," she answered Tina.

The girls finished sewing their shoes. Gina got ready to go home.

Tina checked the street out the window. "Gina, it is dark outside. Nick will walk you home."

"Tina, it's hardly dark at all! Besides, Nick is working on an invention. I'll be home in thirty seconds." Gina dashed out of the apartment and ran the few steps to her home. She didn't want to walk with Nick. "I just can't concentrate on Max when I'm with Nick!" she thought.

She climbed the stairs and safely entered the cozy apartment. Her uncle, Sugarplum, and Valerya Isodorovna were there to greet her.

Chapter Twenty

Gina hated school more each time she entered the grey and olive green classrooms. She studied ballet at the academy, but she studied academics at the International School. Academic courses at the ballet academy were taught only in Russian. Gina thought that math was hard enough when it was taught in English. School was almost out for the year. Gina was restless and irritable.

Gina didn't talk to any of the diplomats' kids. Gina watched them with their heads together. They complained about Russian food and their small apartments. They complained about the lack of amusement parks, pop music, American television, and fast food restaurants. They complained until the instructor appeared and class began.

Not any of them had ever worked as hard at anything as Gina did at ballet. Gina participated in class. She did her part when the students broke up into groups to do tasks. Other than that she kept to herself.

During a study break Gina finished her homework. She thought about how she liked Russian television. She started sketching characters from cartoons. She drew the little hedgehog, the big bear, and the fox. The cartoons were charming and funny. The Russian words didn't prevent her from understanding the simple stories for children.

Gina had come to regard Russian as a pretty language, at least of Leningraders. Women on the streets or in shops sounded like chattering, fluttering birds. The men sounded like trains rushing along a track. They did not sound like the heavier, duller, slower, Moscow accent that she heard on television news programs. Russian spoken by her ballet instructors was like whispering, or dry leaves rustling, clear and soft. Gina liked it.

One morning Gina looked over at her uncle sipping his coffee. "Uncle Gene, can't I just study with you and Tina?" She shifted slightly in her creaky wooden dining room chair. She added sugar to her tea.

"I am glad to hear you ask. Though I suspect it has more to do with your lack of feeling for the International School, than regard for me as a teacher," he smiled back.

Gina ignored his comments. "I can do math with Tina, and English literature and everything else with you. Then I wouldn't have to go to that school at all! You might as well know, Tina would be thrilled if you did English grammar with both of us."

"Perfect!" he grinned, "Saturday and Sunday mornings, then, with recitations in the early evenings?"

"Uncle Gene, No! Not morning. Besides, we have ballet class Saturday mornings," Gina reminded him.

"Oh, we shall do everything in the evening then. I will work up a syllabus. We will begin immediately," he planned.

"Thank heaven for that," thought Gina. She was unhappy at the International School. Gene had tried hard to make everything nice for her here in Leningrad. She tried especially long and hard to like it. Now she didn't have to go back there! She could finish eighth grade under the direction of her uncle.

And double thank heaven for Tina suggesting that they study with Gene together. That way Gina wouldn't feel boxed in and try to be perfect for her uncle. Some of the attention would be cast on Tina. And triple thank heaven that Tina hated memorizing poetry as much as Gina did.

Together that evening in the living room, they convinced Dr. Shostek how they should study. Gina perched on the arm of the sofa next to where her uncle was sitting. "Uncle Gene, the best way to learn English grammar is to write our own poetry, short stories, and plays."

Tina stood in front of Gene pacing back and forth as she made her plea. "Professor Shostek, Gina has point. It not so good only to memorize poems. We will not understand meaning."

Gina put her arm around her uncle's shoulder. "Yes, Uncle Gene, Tina is right! And after we write stuff, our favorite professor can make corrections."

"All right girls. We will try this. You will write one play, poem, or story. I will correct the grammar. Then you must perform it for me and Tina's family," he smiled.

"Uncle Gene, that is so great!" Gina hugged her uncle's shoulder.

"Professor Shostek, what wonderful idea you have!" Tina clapped her hands.

Gina and Tina danced off to Gina's room. First they stopped in the kitchen for cookies, jam, crackers, apples, and hot tea. They spread their picnic around the tiny room. Gina told Tina about Gabriela.

Tina spread jam on a cracker. "Who is Gabriela? Is she person you know? An aunt?"

Gina poured tea for both of them. "No, my mother and I made her up. Well, first mom made her up when she told me bedtime stories. Then I helped make up the stories."

Tina mumbled through her cracker, "What are stories about?"

Tina raised her eyebrows as Gina stirred a hill of sugar into her tea. "Gabriela has wonderful adventures. At the end of every story she is returned to her home by a titled prince, or an eccentric scientist. Or by a fascinating spy, and put safely to bed. It was really cute how mom did that, having them all end up with Gabriela falling asleep."

"And you still make up stories before bed?" Tina asked.

"Sometimes. Usually I just think abut my mom while I'm falling asleep." Tina looked in horror as Gina happily sipped her super-sweetened tea.

"Yes, Gina, that is good thing to do," Tina gently said. "Making up stories is much fun! May I make up someone?"

"You have to make up someone Tina! That's the whole idea!"

Tina thought for a moment as she spread jam on a second cracker. "My friend will be called Cecily. She is friend to Gabriela."

"Cecily! What a great name! Terrific!" The girls started their work. Gina had notebooks, pens, and crayons ready for them. The crayons were to draw ideas for sets, props, and costumes.

"Tina, I think our first play should be about Cecily and Gabriela going on a trip."

Tina nodded. "Oh, yes! But, where? To Paris? To London? Vienna?"

"All of those places! Let's have them tour with a ballet company. Both will dance as prima ballerina. The audiences will be SRO!" Gina dramatically threw up her hand for emphasis.

"Gina, what is SRO? I don't think we have in Russia."

Gina was wildly scribbling notes. "It means Standing Room Only. You know, some people have to stand because all of the seats are sold out. Cecily and Gabriela will get wonderful reviews in the newspapers. They'll be interviewed on T.V."

Tina looked to the ceiling and sighed. "They will be invited to be in movies with handsome actors."

"I thought you didn't have time for boys?" Gina frowned.

"I don't. Cecily does." Tina lifted her nose on the air as she picked up a cup of tea.

"Very funny. Let's get a draft done for my uncle so we can perform soon!" The girls dove into writing their very first play.

From above, Lily scratched her head and thought a bit. Each time the girls tried to write that either Cecily or Gabriela was falling in love with a prince or movie star, Lily kicked over a cup of tea. The girls shrieked and quickly wiped it up. Lily darted around the room, satisfied that she could guide the young playwrights away from too much interest in boys!

That weekend Gene read the play and returned it to the girls to fix their mistakes. The girls corrected the grammar and spelling as he suggested. The girls rehearsed for a week in the living room. Once they were ready to perform the play, they invited Tim, Lena, Misha, Nick, Ilya Alexandrovich, and Tatiana Ivanovna to Gene and Gina's apartment. They invited Tina's grandparents, although they knew no English. Harry, who worked alongside Gene at the consulate, came as well.

The girls performed their play in the living room. They played all the parts themselves. Gina even played the part of an Airedale whom Cecily met on the street and invited into their hotel. Tina especially enjoyed playing waiters, bellhops, directors, double-agents. She liked to play any part that required a deep voice and a fake mustache.

In the second act Gina/Gabriela stood stock still playing a lonely street lamp. Tina/Cecily cried under the streetlamp. The charming, dashing young prince with whom Cecily had fallen madly in love could not marry her. She was not of royal blood. He could only marry a princess. Gina wrinkled her nose. She smelled the scent of her mother's *Joy* perfume wafting down to her.

Everyone loved the play. The audience clapped loudly at the end. They had refreshments in the dining room. After everyone was gone, Gene and Gina cleared away dishes and took them to the kitchen.

"The oddest thing happened during the play." Gene turned on the tap to run over the plates.

"What, Uncle Gene?" Gina carefully ran water into the delicate teacups to rinse them.

Gene started drying dishes with a towel. "I thought I heard your mother laugh. And there was a note of Lily's perfume in the air. I am sure I was only imagining..."

Gina stopped what she was doing and turned to look at him. "No, Uncle Gene, I smelled the perfume, too!"

Gene was drying saucers. "I suppose one of the women in the room has the same perfume."

Gina stood firm. "Oh, no they don't. I asked Tina. Not one store has *Joy* anywhere in Leningrad. They only have Russian perfumes with Russian names."

Lily softly giggled behind her hand. She floated from the kitchen back to Gina's bedroom.

Gene patted Gina's shoulder. "Perhaps we were both remembering Lily tonight. She would have loved the play. Sweet dreams, Gina."

"Night, Uncle Gene." Gina smiled at him and went to her room.

Gina thought about how much fun she had doing the play. She got ready for bed. "I had so much fun performing. I wasn't nervous at all. Maybe it's because I wasn't dancing. And it wasn't in a real theater," she thought. "Or maybe it has something to do with telling a story, like Ilya Alexandrovich said," she wondered. She drifted off to sleep.

Chapter Twenty-One

Several evenings later the girls were in Tina's room getting ready to write a new play. Gina recalled her mom telling her about going to the State Fair in Minnesota. The girls decided to write their new play about it. Gina told Tina the story about her mom and Aunt Maggie going to the Minnesota State Fair. Tina took up her pen and wrote.

Early on in the story Tina looked up. "Oh, can I play your mother's sister, your Aunt Maggie?"

"That would be fine! Do you think you could get Nick to build something for us that looks like the Space Needle ride in the story?" Gina asked hopefully.

Tina stopped writing for a moment. "Yes, I think Nick could do. He shall do anything for you, Gina!"

Gina frowned slightly at Tina, but then smiled. She continued the story. "When Aunt Maggie, Uncle Gene, and my mom were kids, they went to the Minnesota State Fair. They looked at award-winning jellies, crocheted comforters, and flower arrangements. They ooed and ahhed over baby lambs. They looked at bunnies, poultry, and the five hundred pound sow. My mom and Aunt Maggie crowed along with the roosters in the poultry barn. My grandfather made them stop. He said there was enough chicken noise without them adding to it."

Tina scribbled furiously. "Gina, slow, please. I do not know all words. How much did pig weigh?"

"Five hundred pounds," Gina answered and waited while Tina caught up.

Gina continued, "They waited in line for ice-cream cones. They bought them in the Dairy Building. There they had busts of the girls who were State Fair Princesses. The princesses had to sit for hours in a glassed-in refrigerator with a sculptor. They sat in the cold wearing their rhinestone tiaras and satin sashes while their likenesses were carved into large blocks of butter. Mom and Aunt Maggie stood outside and made faces at the poor things."

"Princesses! It does not seem they were cared for like princesses! Statues of butter? And you think Russians do strange things," Tina remarked.

Gina thought for a second. "I guess it is a little strange. Anyway, mom and Aunt Maggie had more fun than that."

Gina went on to describe Machinery Hill, where her grandfather and her Uncle Gene liked to look at tractors and combines. "My mom and Aunt Maggie planned their escape to the Midway. There they rode roller coasters and Ferris wheels that made you sick, unless you were one of the Notorious and Fearless Shostek Sisters."

"Notorious and Fearless Shostek Sisters? What is that?" Tina stopped to cross out a wrong word and erase.

"That's what they called themselves. I suppose it's like when we call ourselves Cecily and Gabriela." Gina glanced over at Tina's notes. "It's spelled N-O-T-O-R-I-O-U-S, not N-A-T-O-R-I-Y-U-S."

Tina nodded and fixed the word again. Gina went on to tell her about the Space Needle ride on the edge of the State Fair grounds that could be seen from anywhere. "The family rule was, 'If you get lost, meet at the Space Needle,'" Gina explained. "The Space Needle is the dullest ride at the fair. You sit inside this tower that goes around about as fast as a glacier melting. It goes up about an foot an hour until you are high enough to see the whole fairgrounds. No one ever goes on it, so there's no crowd around it."

"That is what you want Nick to build?" Tina made a sketch of the Space Needle as Gina described it.

Gina looked it over. "Yes! Your drawing looks just like it! I want Nick to build a small one, just sort of a model. Anyway, my mom suggested to Aunt Maggie giving Gene and their parents the slip early in the day. She grabbed Aunt Maggie's arm. They raced off to see sideshows with bearded ladies, fire-eating men, and live snakes."

"Oh, I want to play bearded lady, too!" Tina went to the mirror and drew on a beard with eyeliner. She turned for Gina's approval.

"Tina, sometimes you are so weird." Gina rolled her eyes.

"I am not weird, only artistic," Tina sniffed.

Gina smiled. "From there they went to the funhouses and on the scariest rides. My Aunt Maggie worried all the way. Aunt Maggie begged and begged mom to go back so they wouldn't get in trouble. Mom shushed her. They ate forbidden cotton candy that was the worst thing in the world for their teeth.

"This is true! It is very bad for teeth!" Tina interrupted.

Gina shushed her and continued. "Mom and Aunt Maggie finally went back to the entrance of the Space Needle. Their parents and Gene were calmly waiting on a bench eating Minnesota apples. My mom breathlessly made up a story of how they had lost track of time in the 4-H Building. They were looking at the butterfly and rock collections. Luckily, the 4-H Building had the same rock and butterfly exhibits year in and year out. It made my grandparents happy that their daughters took an interest in science. My mom replied, 'Why, yes, papa, the Lepidoptera were most beautiful this time.' She elbowed my aunt in the ribs.

Aunt Maggie said, 'Yes, and the striation in the igneous rocks was the best we've ever seen!'"

"Gina, this will make great play! We can get cotton candy from circus and use it in performance."

"Hey, that's a great idea! Plus we'll get to see the circus!" The girls continued writing until Tatiana Ivanovna came in. She said that she had telephoned Uncle Gene. Gina was allowed to spend the night. Then she told them to go to sleep!

Chapter Twenty-Two

Gina and Tina awakened early the next morning. The students at the academy were preparing for end-of-year recitals. Tina and Gina quickly ate breakfast. They raced off to ballet class and rehearsal. Tina's recital in the Russian Division was to be held first at the Kirov Theater. Gina's recital for the International Division was to be held later in the Palace of Culture on Nevsky Avenue.

In the Russian Division, Tina had already passed all of her examinations, both academic and artistic. Aside from regular exams in math, science, Russian literature, and grammar, Tina had a two-hour-long exam in ballet. She showed how well she executed each step that she had learned that year and all the years before. She performed well and was promoted to the next level.

In the International Division, Gina had completed her ballet exam. She also had done quite well alongside the other girls. Both girls had been nervous about their exams. The instructors from the upper levels judged them, as well as their own teacher. Not all girls passed. Some, who had not worked hard enough, or who did not have the temperament required to be a ballerina, were asked to leave the academy.

Generally, only children born with the kind of body needed for a professional career were accepted into the academy. Occasionally a pretty or musical child was accepted. The commission had hopes that she might develop other strengths. She might have a career as a folk dancer, or perhaps as a dancer for background scenes in the opera. Sometimes the commission realized they had made a mistake in accepting such a girl and she was not promoted to the next level. There was a great amount of relief among students judged good enough to continue to study at the academy.

On an evening late in May, Gina went to the Kirov Theater to watch Tina dance in her recital. Tina was the only girl in Level Four to be given one of the fairy variations in *The Sleeping Beauty*. The other fairy solos were given to girls from Level Five or above. All of the girls at the academy were jealous of Tina. Gina could feel it.

After she was cast in the part, Tina blithely went about school, dancing, working hard, being kind and helpful. Gina looked around the rehearsal hall. The parents and siblings of the boys and girls who would perform were allowed to be there right before the performance began. Gina knew the moment Tina was on stage which ones would begin to whisper about Tina. They would not say nice things at all.

Gina left the humming room and followed a maze of hallways. She headed to the room where Tina was making-up and dressing. Gina wanted to stop the other girls from talking. She did in a way. As she walked past the other girls they stopped whispering. They knew she was Tina's friend. They looked at her out of the corners of their eyes and went back to putting on make-up. It agitated Gina to think of her friend being talked about in an unkind manner.

Gina could not have stood it herself. She realized that was part of why she didn't want to dance on stage. She deeply feared the meanness of other girls. Gina feared their unkind comments. She knew she might get hurt by girls saying mean things if she danced in front of an audience. She pushed that out of her mind.

She made her way past the last few tiny rooms. Girls sat hunched over their paints straining toward the mirrors. Some sewed last minute ribbons on pointe shoes. Some were wetting down stray wisps of hair.

"Tina, aren't you scared?" asked Gina. She came up behind Tina's wooden chair.

"No," Tina blinked.

"Isn't what the other girls are saying bothering you?" pressed Gina.

"I have not heard them. What do they say?" Tina brushed her hair up into a ponytail, in preparation for pinning it into a bun.

Gina helped Tina put the elastic band around the ponytail. "That you are too young for this part. That you only get to do it because your father is the artistic director."

"That. Nothing new. Gina, people talk about all girls who have big role. Every time. In all of history. Not only about me. It does not hurt me. Such talk only hurts girls who say those things. I can only do what I am here to do. I cannot spend time to help those girls." Together they started pinning Tina's hair into a bun.

"Help them! Why would you want to help them? I want to slug them!" exclaimed Gina.

"Because they are sad," Tina explained. "People who are happy or who are working have no time for meanness." "People talking about her hurt my mother," Gina said. "Many women were jealous of her. They were very mean to her."

"I know what it is like to hear cruel girls talk, but I must keep myself strong to do what I must do. Now leave me please, Gina. I get ready!" Tina waved Gina away.

Lily floated nearby and listened to the Gina and Tina talking. "I remember those jealous, hurtful girls. Gina, I wish upon you a gentle calm." With a little wave of her hand she followed Gina into the theater.

Gina sat down in her seat as the ballet began. Tina danced like light skittering across the ocean. Gina was happy that Tina had chosen her as her friend. She wondered if she would ever be happy dancing in front of an audience. Tina was elated to dance for so many people.

Suddenly Tina's pink shoe slipped slightly from underneath her. She wobbled, and nearly fell. She regained her footing and went on to finish her dance. Gina was embarrassed for her. "How awful. Tina must feel terrible," she thought. The applause for Tina was very loud. Gina thought it was to make Tina feel better and that people felt sorry for her.

After the performance Gina went to the dressing room. Tina was changing her clothes. "I'm so sorry, Tina! You almost fell!"

Tina was smiling into the mirror. She quickly removed her make up. "It is good, Gina! I was pretending to be real fairy! I felt like I could fly! It was wonderful feeling! I will never forget." She looked up at Gina with a glowing face.

Gina was confused. "But you almost fell! Isn't that wrong?"

“Gina, I am in academy. I am student. Academy is where we learn to go beyond self, to fall, to get up, and go on! Gina, I near forgot to tell you! Papa wants you to dance solo in White Nights Festival in summer! Many artists from Kirov and from all over world perform short pieces. You will be beautiful!" Tina packed the last of her things into a dance bag.

"Wait! What! I can't dance a solo! What's the White Nights Festival?" Gina walked with Tina back into the lobby. Tina did not have a chance to answer because so many people rushed up to congratulate her. They told her how beautifully she had danced.

Gina thought in disbelief, “She made a mistake! She almost fell! And everyone still thinks she is great! That is so unfair! I never make mistakes and no one thinks I’m great. I'll be awful in a solo.”

Gina thought about this all the way home and on into the apartment. In her prayers she asked Lily to help her figure it out.

Lily gazed down from the ceiling, sending her daughter thoughts. “Silly, Gina! Ilya Alexandrovich gives you private lessons! You are a student at the Kirov Academy! Many people think you are great. Soon, you will know it, too.”

Chapter Twenty-Three

Tina and Gina set down their pens in triumph one afternoon. "We're done!" They hugged each other and looked over their work. For their final examination for Dr. Shostek, they had written their best play so far. In the play, Cecily and Gabriela left home and were touring the world. They were appearing in a ballet called *The Clown, the Lady in Red, and 500 Pairs of Shoes*.

They performed in the most beautiful cities in Europe. Cecily and Gabriela danced for audiences in London, Amsterdam, Vienna, and Rome. Lastly they danced in Paris, the City of Lights. Tina and Gina spent hours with encyclopedias researching the wonderful places. They wrote descriptive passages about each place. Dr. Shostek surely would be impressed, they thought.

"Gina, we shall practice *The Clown, the Lady in Red, and 500 Pairs of Shoes* more times before we show to your uncle, yes? I want to be sure it is good."

"Yes, this will be great, Tina. We get to play Cecily and Gabriela traveling all over the world. We even get to pretend we are them performing in a show! I think Uncle Gene's going to love it," Gina said. She took out her ballet slippers.

The girls rehearsed. Gene came by several times to see what all the laughing was about. They shut the door to him each time he tried to enter.

The Clown, the Lady in Red, and 500 Pairs of Shoes
A Tragic Comedy or Comic Tragedy in Three Acts

Act I

The scene opens with a lonely clown onstage. He is dressed in white with black ruffles around his neck and wrists and ankles. He is sad and alone and has no friends. He dances a sad dance to sad violin music.

A Spanish lady in a beautiful red dress sees him. She dances for him to cheer him up. He watches her dance and is frightened. He is colorblind. He thinks that she is a large green alligator. He runs away.

The Lady in Red thinks that he does not like her dancing. She stops dancing. She begins to cry. She runs away.

Act II

Five cobblers come onto the stage. They set up their benches. They begin slowly to make shoes. Two hundred and fifty beautiful ladies and two hundred and fifty handsome men come onto the stage. They are wearing red, blue, green, purple, yellow, and orange costumes.

The beautiful ladies and handsome men dance about in excitement. They are to perform a ballet that evening. Their shoes are not ready. They dance and they argue. They plead with the cobblers to finish their shoes in time for the show.

The cobblers work at their craft. They shake their heads when the dancers say they must work faster, faster! The cobblers know that good shoes are made with time and care.

The Sad Clown returns as the last of the shoes are being made. Arguments begin over which shoes look best with which costumes. The dancers grab shoes from each other to try on with their costumes. They push and pull shoes back and forth from each other. The cobblers try to break up the fights over the shoes.

The Spanish Lady in the Red Dress wanders back on stage. She sees the cobblers. She sees the dancers ask the Sad Clown what shoes should go with which costumes. The five cobblers, two hundred and fifty beautiful ladies, and two hundred and fifty handsome men ask the Sad Clown to settle the fight.

Act III

The Sad Clown is frightened. All of the costumes and shoes look the same color to him. The Spanish Lady understands that he is color-blind. The Sad Clown bravely tells them his secret. He asks the cobblers to decide which shoes go with which costumes.

All step back as the Spanish Lady dances for the Sad Clown again. He dances for her. They dance together. They fall in love.

The five hundred dancers don their new shoes with help from the cobblers. They dance a finale. The cobblers fall asleep from exhaustion at having made so many shoes in one afternoon.

The End

The girls finished practicing. They sat on the floor eating grapes and crackers. That was all they found in the cupboard that day.

Tina took a small bunch of grapes. "Gina, it is great play. It will be fun to pretend we are Cecily and Gabriela in Paris in ballet. It would be good if I could travel as you do." "I haven't been anywhere!"

Gina was half way in her closet looking for clothes that they could use as costumes for the play.

"Gina, you are here! Long, long way from home," Tina reminded her.

Gina said from the closet. "There is no way I have enough shoes for this play. We'll have to use some of your shoes, too." Tina nodded.

Gina emerged from the closet with five pairs of shoes. "I know I am a long way from home, but it doesn't seem like traveling to stay put in one place. I mean, we don't go on bus tours and buy postcards and stuff." Tina offered Gina grapes. She shook her head, "No."

Tina separated some grapes from their stems. "I have only traveled in own country. Even so it is difficult to get visa. The government likes all time to know where we are. Papa took us to Alma-Ata last year. It was very difficult to arrange."

"Where's Alma-Ata?" Gina asked.

"It is capital city of Kazakhstan. It is near to China. Papa has friend there. She trains to be opera singer. We went to visit her and husband. And we all went to see National Kazakh Ballet. It was wonderful, Gina! The girls are all Kazakh. They are tall and dark and mysterious. They are powerful, not like little ballerina dolls." Tina stood as she spoke. She walked majestically around the room to demonstrate.

Gina turned back to the closet. "I thought you loved being a ballerina."

"I do. It is my life. I want to show ballet is powerful in my life. I want to show ballet is powerful to other people. That is what I want for life, Gina. Not to show ballerina as fairy, or angel, or doll. I want to dance as real girl with real problems who is strong and who helps self."

"You sure read a lot into this stuff, don't you? I don't think about that when I dance." Gina held up a pinkish shirt and skirt for Tina's approval for the Lady in Red.

Tina shrugged and went to the closet to help Gina.

"What do you think about when you dance, Gina?"

"I think about how many mistakes I'm going to make!" Gina handed a red sweatshirt to Tina.

"Oh, Gina! You are fine! Still, I wish I could travel way you do. To pack bags, show passport, and to go!" Tina took the red sweatshirt and put it on the pile of possible costumes on the bed.

"You can't?" Gina was shocked.

"No, we must wait in line for hours to get visa, tickets, all. It takes much time. There was time when we could not at all travel." Tina sat on the bed and explained.

"Is that why Rudolph Nureyev and Mikhail Baryshnikov came to America? My mother told me it was in all the newspapers. The whole world was shocked. My teacher, Madame Branitskaya, was on tour with Baryshnikov when he left. She could not believe he went to the U.S. But then later she moved to the U.S., too." Gina said.

"Nureyev and Baryshnikov wanted to see world, to dance for world. They left Russia against government. Government will not let family and friends in Russia talk to them ever again. Not even letters. They cannot ever come back to visit mothers or families. Not ever," Tina said.

Gina said, "Madame Branitskaya said that she happier in the U.S., but that she misses her mother."

Tina sighed, "Sometimes I think I want to leave and dance all over world! But it is best to wait until I graduate from academy. Then I can dance wherever I want. If I can work for troupe outside Russia I can travel freely."

"I don't know if I'm going to end up dancing anywhere, Tina, not wherever I want." Gina sat on the bed next to Tina

"Oh, Gina. Think better of self! Papa says you make much progress. He asked you to dance in White Nights Festival. That is big thing. Papa has had many foreign students. You are first American he asked to dance in festival." Tina pawed through scarves and hats and gloves on the bed looking for the right accessories for the characters in their play. "Really? The first American? I wonder why he asked me? I still don't know if I want to dance in the festival or not." Gina looked at her pointe shoes on the nightstand.

"He picked you because you are good, silly! And because you learn! And you face fear. Papa loves to see others learn. You must dance in festival. It is great honor to be chosen by papa. It is very rude if you do not dance," Tina explained.

"Oh, all right. I'll dance in the festival. But, why can't everyone else learn for a while and me just stay the way I am? I'm tired of learning and changing and facing my fears for everyone else. I'm still as scared as I've always been." Gina put a hunter's cap of her uncle's with ear-flaps on her head and made a face.

Tina laughed, but turned serious. "There is secret to getting over fear! You must do it for self."

"I know you're right," Gina sighed and took off the cap.

"Come, let's rehearse again. You play Sad Clown this time. He faces big fear in play when he comes back to Spanish Lady!" Tina jumped up from the bed.

"Who'd be afraid of cobblers and a bunch of dancers?" Gina crunched on a cracker.

"Gina, it is Sad Clown's role and character to be afraid and then to get over fear. Practice!"

"All right, all right already." Gina put a fluffy scarf around her neck in place of the clown's ruffled collar and the girls started the play.

They finished rehearsing. Gina and Tina sat on the floor laughing. "Tina, you were right. It is good to play someone getting over fear. That was fun!"

"I thought you might think so. I go home for dinner now. Papa will be watching for me." Gina walked Tina to the door of the apartment.

"Bye, Tina. And thank you!" Gina skipped off to her room.

In her room, Gina went over the steps for the recital for the International Division that was coming up. She didn't feel like she was getting over fear when she practiced for the recital. She felt like she was making the fear get bigger. She still worried about getting sick at the recital.

Even though Lily breathed calm, loving thoughts down to Gina, she had trouble sleeping.

Chapter Twenty-Four

The following morning Gina practiced for her recital for the International Division of the academy. Gina was one of the four little swans from *Swan Lake.* In a few days she would perform it with three of the other students in the third level. It was a recital like Tina's in the Russian Division at the Kirov Theater, except Gina's would be performed in a theater smaller than the Kirov.

The four swans danced with their arms intertwined with each other's. The girls were exactly the same height. They must perform the dance without error. Any mistake would throw off the other girls. Her teacher had assigned Gina the part so that the other swans could drag Gina on stage if necessary. Gina loved the dance. She hated the intertwining arms part. It was so uncomfortable.

Gina was practicing in Gene's study. She was frustrated. She thought that practicing in a room that she didn't normally dance in might help. Even Sugarplum wouldn't listen to Gina complaining anymore. "I just don't have courage. Fine, so I don't dance with passion! When I dance with passion I make mistakes! I can't do both, be perfect and dance with emotion. Cowardly Lion, yes, I am!" Sugarplum turned and left the room.

She was trying to use her mother's story about the forest to tell a story with her dance. Gina thought about The Man with Fire in His Eyes and about Max when she danced. She tried dancing the piece again. It didn't seem to make any difference. "I still am freaked out," she thought.

She turned from her piece for the recital to the piece for the White Nights Festival. That performance was in two weeks. The White Nights Festival lasted over several evenings at the Kirov Theater. One evening was devoted to ballet, one to theater, and one to orchestral music. There were other performances of opera and poetry.

It was not a student recital. It was her debut as an almost-professional ballerina. She would be dancing a solo. In the program she would be listed as a Guest Artist from the United States.

Ilya Alexandrovich had not asked Gina if she would do the solo. He told her that she was going to do it. The stage manager would push her out of the wings onto the stage if need be. If she felt sick, there would be a bucket and towels nearby. She had no out.

The music and piece for the White Nights Festival was difficult. Ilya Alexandrovich had choreographed it for her. The music was Maurice Ravel's *Pavane pour une Infante defunte.* The title meant, "Dance for a Dead Princess." It reminded Gina of Lily. She supposed that was why Ilya Alexandrovich had chosen it for her.

The choreography had to be danced technically beautifully. It had to be danced with a deep emotional quality. She must express sadness and joy in one short solo. If she didn't, it would appear immature and silly. Gina went over the steps several times. She decided to take a break.

Gina looked around the study. This small room was covered with cream and gold striped wallpaper. It contained a small wooden desk. There was not one personal item of her uncle's, other than books and papers.

Gene hadn't brought any pictures of his family with him to Russia. There were no photos of his parents, or of his sisters, on his desk or on the walls.

Gene had left the arrangement of the apartment to Valerya Isidorovna and Gina. The two of them tried to make the place warm and colorful. Valerya Isidorovna brought plants in boxes. They were supposed to flower in the window sills. For some reason they never bloomed. Now they were buried behind the many books and newspapers that occupied Gene's time each day. Gina went to her room and returned with a framed photograph of her grandparents, Lily, Maggie, and Gene. She placed it on Gene's desk.

There were scribbled bits of paper everywhere. Gina knew that Gene wanted to write a book. He told Gina he wanted to write foreign language dictionaries. Not the standard Russian to English, or English to Russian dictionaries. He wanted to write obscure combinations, like Russian to Japanese, or Amharic to Russian.

Gina found him a few times, paging through medical or technical dictionaries. He wrote words in lists that he thought he might use someday. She told him he would drive himself crazy. She made him stop by taking the dictionaries away into her room. She insisted that she needed them for her homework.

Gina rested more in the living room. Gene came home from work and saw her on the sofa.

"Uncle Gene, let's go for a walk. If I rehearse anymore today, I'll go crazy." Gina looked up at him.

"It is a fine day. The weather is clear and bright. I will get a notebook." Gene put his jacket back on and started for his study.

Gina shook her head, "No, not today, Uncle Gene. No note taking, no lessons, no books. You may bring one map with you. This is a walk for fun!"

"All right then, Gina. I shall follow wherever you lead!" They ran down the stairs and into the courtyard.

They walked from the apartment along Rubinstein Street. They took a left out onto Nevsky Avenue. Nevsky was named after the Neva River that flowed across Leningrad. They crossed over a bridge. Leningrad was like the Italian city of Venice. Like Venice, it had many canals and beautiful bridges throughout the city. An Italian, Rastrelli, had designed Leningrad under the direction of Peter the Great, one of the first tsars of Russia.

"Gina, I saved this walking map from my first time in Leningrad. I was studying at the university. Look at this. We are walking on Marata Street. Here on the map it says we are on Zodchenko Street. Russian maps contain many errors! Maps created for foreigners are drawn to lead tourists away from military bases, nuclear power plants, or secret revolutionary hideouts."

"If all of the maps are wrong, why do they make them? Is it a spy thing?" Gina jumped over a small puddle left from a recent rain.

"Yes. It is also to fool spies who are trying discover military secrets. When I was a student I walked all over the city noting the errors on the maps. It interested me."

Gene looked around to see if anyone was watching and then jumped over the puddle himself. "Now I note the errors because the street names are changing again as the government is changing. It is included in my daily report to Washington, D.C."

"That's what you do at the consulate? You tell them how everything around here is changing?" Gina buttoned her coat around her neck. There was a cool breeze.

"Each day I gather information on the changing political situation. I use every newspaper, wire service, radio, or television transmission that I can find. I put that together with the information from the meetings I attend pretending to be a Russian." Gene tried to put the scarf he had around his neck on Gina's head, but she waved it away.

"When you wear the spy costume?" Gina asked.

"It is not a spy costume, but yes, when I dress as a Russian citizen. I write a report on Russia's shifting power structure. I send it to Washington, D.C. every afternoon." Gene folded the woolen scarf and put it in his pocket.

"Sounds like you're in school, Uncle Gene. Except you give yourself homework to do. I don't understand what shifting power structure is. What's the report about?" Gina sidestepped several people on the sidewalk hurrying home from work.

Gene kept an arm on Gina's shoulder so he wouldn't lose track of her. "I report which officials in power are losing their jobs. I report if any officials are moving into new positions. And I report on officials that have simply disappeared."

"Disappeared? You sound like a spy again, Uncle Gene."

"Yes, disappeared. In hiding. Trying to leave the country. Perhaps, dead." Gene pulled her a little closer to him.

Gina looked up at him with concern. "Gosh, Uncle Gene."

"It is a very serious situation. As soon as I make the report to Washington, D.C., I know by the next morning everything will have changed." Gene sighed.

"Uncle Gene, this is really hard for me to understand," said Gina.

"I know, my dear. I confess, I do not understand all of it myself." Gene pointed toward the park and they continued down Nevsky Avenue toward it until the huge statue of a woman came into view. "There is the monument to Catherine the Great. She was the first tsaritsa of Russia."

"I know, Velarya Isidorovna told me. She's so homely, but the park is nice." Gina waved at the statue.

Gene steered Gina away from the park and they crossed Nevsky Avenue. "I do not know that it is an exact likeness of her. I do not imagine too many people look attractive carved out of stone. So, you and Valerya Isidorovna have had a few conversations in Russian, it seems."

"Yes, it seems." Gina quickly changed the subject. "Oh, look! Passage! It's Tina's favorite store. She doesn't like to shop. She just thinks it's pretty."

They entered. It was made of cream-colored marble. It had staircases with black, curled iron railings. There was a space in the middle that went all the way up to the arched, third floor ceiling. Small bridges connected the many clothing stores from one side of the building to the other. They exited and crossed Nevsky Avenue.

They entered the other large yellow and white shopping complex, Gostiny Dvor. It, too, was three stories high. It had marble staircases and hallways with dozens of chandeliers. The stores were beautiful. But there were few things to buy, clothing and kitchenware mainly. The items for sale were of poor quality and cheaply made. The best quality products were exported and sold in other countries.

They went on to Dom Knigy a little way down Nevsky Avenue. Gene told Gina, "Dom Knigy is a bookstore. It used to sell old political posters. For kopecks one could buy large, white and red posters with Nikolai Lenin's face. On it would be a slogan such as, 'Workers of the World, Unite!'"

They looked into the nearly empty bins. A few of the old time posters remained. Gina looked at one of Lenin, a former leader of Russia. "Don't you think he looks like Colonel Sanders? You know, the chicken guy?"

Gene examined the poster. "Funny. He does bear a resemblance. I never noticed that before."

They walked past the beautiful Our Lady of Kazan Cathedral. "In the evenings people gather outside the Kazan to openly discuss the political situation. They can gather and talk without fear of arrest," Gene remarked.

The square in front of the Kazan was filled with singers, mimes, painters, and poets. They were there freely performing their art. No longer censored by the government, the artists painted, said, wrote, or danced, whatever they pleased. They stopped momentarily and watched a mime perform.

Gina whispered to Gene. "Uncle Gene, I can't tell what he's miming. I don't think he's very good."

He whispered back, "I cannot tell what he is doing either. Freedom does not necessarily guarantee quality of art, I am afraid."

Gina held her uncle's elbow. "You know, I wish you came to the Kazan only in the daytime. It's too dangerous at night."

Gene shook his head. "It is my job, Gina. I must do it well."

Gina and Gene ended their tour at the Hermitage Museum. Gene waved his arm grandly to point it out to Gina. "The Hermitage Museum used to be the Winter Palace of the tsars of Russia. It is bordered on one side by Palace Square. See the high, slender column of the Alexandrine monument in the center."

Gina laughed. "That Alexandrine monument thing reminds me of the Space Needle at the State Fair. But it doesn't have the part that people sit in to ride."

"The Alexandrine monument was named after Emperor Alexander I. He led Russia to win a war over France. As you can see, the Hermitage Museum is bordered on the other side by the Neva River." They walked across the square. It was full of tour buses, ice cream kiosks, and families with children.

Inside the museum they looked at paintings by Picasso, Corot, Monet, and Degas. They looked at sculptures by Rodin and Michaelangelo. They looked at gold, silver, and gem-encrusted gifts from foreign kings to the tsar. They passed through the magnificent throne room of Tsar Nicholas II, the last tsar of Russia.

They gazed in disbelief at the beauty of the rooms Catherine the Great had designed for herself. One set of rooms was in pale pink marble with forty chandeliers. It had a clock shaped like a gigantic golden peacock. More chandeliers hung from balconies that ran around the room. There were carved marble staircases that wound themselves up to the balconies. On the balconies were elegant doors. Those doors led to rooms of richness and splendor.

Gina stopped counting the chandeliers and asked, "How could one person keep all that beauty only for herself?"

"She was showing the world how powerful she was by building these rooms, Gina."

"Couldn't she just have done some push-ups every once in a while?" Gina wandered over to the peacock clock.

"Not that kind of power. Political power." Gene smiled and followed her.

"Yeah, yeah, yeah..." Gina smiled back at him.

The two left at the closing time of the museum. They stopped in at the Café' Literaturnoye. Gene told the waiter in Russian that they needed a table for two. "This was the restaurant in which the poet, Pushkin, had his last dinner before dying in a duel."

"What's a duel?" Gina asked as they waited for a table to be cleared.

Gene answered, "Two men meet in a forest. They stand back to back armed with pistols. They walk away from each other. After a certain number of steps they turn and face one another. They fire their guns. Whoever is left standing wins."

"That's horrible! You mean, they try to kill each other?" Gina followed the waiter and Gene to their table.

"They do," Gene said as they sat down.

"Why the heck would anyone do this duel thing?" Gina wondered to Gene. Gina thanked the waiter in Russian for pushing in her chair. Gene's face was covered in smiles.

"The man who shot Pushkin was having an affair with Pushkin's wife." Gene unfolded his napkin.

"You mean having sex with her behind Pushkin's back?" Gina asked honestly.

Gene cleared his throat. "You expressed it far better than I did. Yes, precisely, having sex with her behind her husband's back." The waiter returned to clear the decorative plates from their table to make room for the regular plates on which their dinner would be served.

"You know, Uncle Gene, people in Hollywood have affairs all the time. They don't shoot each other over it."

"This is true, Gina. It was something that was done in the 1800's."

The waiter returned and served them soup. "That's dumb. But dinner is great. This soup is so good!"

Then Gene ordered shashlik, which was a kind of shishkabob, black caviar, and hot French bread with butter. Gene had a glass of ice-cold vodka. For a time uncle and niece forgot their troubles and the troubles of Russia. They had a wonderful time together.

After ice cream they went to the river and watched the bridges open. The bridges opened at the top to let the tall passing barges go through. The ships and bridges had lights on them. The lights weren't needed.

"It's bright as day, Uncle Gene! And it's ten o'clock at night!"

"That is why it is called White Nights. It will stay light almost all night long. Leningrad is so far north that the sun never sets for two weeks in the summer," Gene said.

"And the festival I will perform in for Ilya Alexandrovich is named for White Nights!" Gina added.

Gene and Gina walked home along Nevsky Avenue. They crossed over the little bridges that crossed the many canals of the old city. They returned to the apartment. Even though it was late, Gina practiced again for her recital. After that, she practiced for the White Nights Festival.

She tried dance the way Ilya Alexandrovich asked her to dance at her lesson the previous day. She tried to think of the story about The Man with Fire in His Eyes. She tried to use ballet to tell the story. She dove in, dancing as passionately as she knew how. She immediately slipped and fell on the polished hardwood floor. She got up and practiced for another hour.

Gene stopped by her room. "Good night, Gina. How is the rehearsing going?"

"Just fine, Uncle Gene, Good night!"

She said her prayers. She asked God and her mother for help to dance better. She fell asleep worrying about her recital for the academy. She feared the White Nights Festival even more.

Lily was still glowing over the wonderful walk and the trip to the Hermitage Museum. "It all was so beautiful!" She twirled and looked down at Gina. "Gina, my dear, I am glad you have this chance to prove yourself! You will dance exquisitely in your recital!"

Chapter Twenty-Five

Gina's recital was to take place at one of the Palaces of Culture in Leningrad. Palaces of Culture were created for nonprofessional artists to learn and perform. In the evenings adults and children went to Palaces of Culture to take dancing, painting, or music lessons. Sometimes Tina went to the Palaces of Culture to perform for children. She also gave ballet lessons to little girls who were not able to study at the academy. The buildings were beautiful. They were filled with marble staircases and high arched ceilings. Each one had a small theater with rows of red velvet seats.

On the day of Gina's recital she met Tina at four in the afternoon. The girls walked the few blocks from the apartment in silence. Tina was gentle with her friend. Tina loved to perform in front of audiences. But she knew that there were many talented and gifted artists who did not. For many performers stage fright was a problem. It was a problem that prevented them from having a professional career.

"Gina, you look especially pretty today," Tina commented. They walked along Nevsky Avenue.

"It's just my old blue skirt and sweater, but thank you, Tina."

"You will dance well today. You are ready!" Tina took her friend's hand and swung her arm.

"Tina, please don't talk to me now. I have to be able to think." Gina shook off Tina's grip.

Tina nodded. "I understand, Gina. I only try to keep you from worry!" They entered the rich and elegant Palace of Culture. Tina hugged Gina and left her to have a cherry compote in the lobby.

Gina went to the dressing room and changed into practice tights and leotard. Then she took her place on stage with the other students from the International Division. The curtains had not yet opened. On stage the ballet mistress led them through a ballet class to warm up.

Gina returned to the dressing room with the other little swans. She put on her make-up, pink tights, white bodice, white tutu, and pointe shoes. She pinned white feathers in her hair. She waited in the wings until it was time to go on. She was frightened, but she didn't feel sick. Gina's teacher had purposely placed her on the inside of the line of four girls. When the time came, the three other little swans, with arms intertwined, pulled Gina onstage.

She thought of the story her mother had written. She thought of the Wind blowing through the trees. She imagined the glints of sun that made their way through the leaves to the floor of the forest. She thought of Wild Friend, who was both Tina and her mother. She danced her steps delicately and flowingly, but strong. She came to a difficult passage in the piece. She imagined the Man with Fire in His Eyes watching her.

Her shoe caught on something in the floor. She stumbled. She fell. Gina brought the other three dancers to the floor with her.

All four girls recovered. They finished the piece perfectly. Gina ran offstage as soon as the lights went to black. She knew she had failed. Afraid to look at Ilya Alexandrovich or her uncle, she ran out of the theater. Tina ran after her.

"Gina, you were wonderful!" Tina breathlessly called. "Don't say it. Don't lie. I was awful and I know it. I'm not going to be a ballerina. I guess I better start liking school. I'll have to figure out something else to be," Gina said. She let Tina catch up to her.

Tina tried to look into Gina's eyes. "Gina, it not your fault! Nail in floor caught pointe shoe! It is fault of stage manager, not your fault! You must believe me!"

Gina avoided Tina's gaze and stared at the floor. "It's not that, Tina. I'm not special, like you are. I'm just plain old boring and scared."

"Gina, it takes time to make great artist. I know this feeling of being special will come to you. Papa does, too." Tina put an arm around her friend. "Come, we go to nursery school to meet Max today."

Gina swirled away from Tina. "Max?! No, I can't! I can't see anyone now. Nursery school?"

"Nursery school. Remember? I told you. I let Max read our play. He wrote music for *The Clown, the Lady in Red, and 500 Pairs of Shoes.* Children in kindergarten are going to perform it. I told you it was today. He will look for us. We must go!" Tina grabbed Gina's arm and pulled her along.

Gina remembered promising to go with Tina to the performance. She felt a sinking feeling in her stomach. She hurried along after her friend.

They reached the door of the school and went up a tiny stairway. It opened onto a large hallway with hooks and cupboards for children's jackets. They passed several rooms filled with brightly colored toys and art materials. Tina led on into a room that had folding chairs set up in rows. There was a curtain across a stage on the far end of the room. The girls found seats in the front row. Many parents and older siblings were there to see the five year-olds perform for the first time.

A very pretty young woman with soft, black curly hair and large dark eyes came out onto the stage. She introduced Max, and announced that the play was beginning. Max played the violin as a five year-old boy playing the Clown danced. Max also played all of the other music pieces throughout the show.

The Clown and the Lady in Red performed their parts solemnly. They seemed quite happy when it was over. The angry cobblers were the funniest part of the show. The chorus of not quite five hundred dancers was a hit.

In the chaos of running children and laughing parents that followed, Tina took Gina's arm again to introduce her to Max. Gina tried to pull away. "Tina, I don't want to meet him!"

Tina kept a firm grip on Gina. "You must! He was very kind to produce our play and write music score. We must thank him." Max stood with his arm around the lovely, dark-haired woman's waist.

"Hello, Gina. You and Tina have written wonderful play. Children and audience are so happy!" Gina figured out that the pretty woman was very special to Max. Gina politely shook hands.

"Your violin playing was wonderful. And the music you wrote for the play was perfect, Maximillien Dmitrievich." She almost called him Moozh. That would have been awful.

Max smiled at Gina. "Gina, I understand you are future ballerina, like Tina."

"Oh, no I'm not!" Gina mumbled. She turned and ran out of the room. This time Tina could not catch up to her. She ran through the streets crying.

Once Gina reached the apartment she stopped crying. She went into her uncle's study. She looked at the picture of her grandparents, Maggie, Gene, and Lily that she had placed on his desk. It was Sunday. Valerya Isidorovna had the day to herself. Gene had not yet returned.

Gina sniffled and looked up from the picture. She thought, "The flowers in that box are finally blooming." She peered into the box on the windowsill. She noticed an envelope that had fallen behind it. She found a letter addressed to her in Lily's handwriting, "For My Daughter, Gina." Gina opened the letter.

Dear Gina,

I miss you, my dear daughter. I miss how you practice your ballet steps every day, even when you don't want to. I miss how you never skip a lesson. I miss how you work hard at memorizing your choreography and perfecting your technique.

Those are the things that make a great artist, Gina. The daily practice, devotion, and love of your art take courage, Gina. You have that!

And you have far more that I never told you. I watched you grow and learn to love ballet. You are talented. I gave you your first ballet shoes because you heard a piece of music played on the radio. You rushed to me so excited, "Mama, what is that beautiful song? I want to dance to that!" I taught you your first steps. I thought how you are my star. You are special and unusual!

I watched you in lessons with Madame Branitskaya. You understood and did everything that she told you to do. You have the temperament of a great artist. You listen to your teachers. You learn from them. Then you go off and make the dance your own. The world is yours, my Gina.

All My Love,

Lily

"Oh, mom. I'm so sorry! I'm not any of those things. And I never will be," Gina sobbed long and hard. Exhausted, she went to her room and fell asleep.

Gene came in later and told her that dinner was ready. He looked at her splotchy face. In a moment he returned with Gina's dinner on a tray. After she finished eating, Gene put his arm around her and told her. "Gina, you performed beautifully at the recital. I saw you rush off with Tina and I could not catch up to tell you."

"I didn't do anything beautifully. I was awful! Why didn't you give me this letter before? I found it in your study," Gina asked. She showed him Lily's letter.

Gene put the dinner tray on the floor and Sugarplum finished Gina's milk. "I do not know about this letter. Where did it come from?"

"It was in the window-sill behind the plants in your den." Gina brushed her hair out of her eyes.

Gene turned the letter over and over. "I do not know how that is possible."

Sugarplum jumped into Gina's arms. "You didn't bring it with you from home? I thought maybe mom wrote it when she was sick and gave it to you to give me."

"No. Lily did not give this to me. I do not know how this letter came to be. It is her handwriting. May I read it?" Gene read the letter. His voice trembled as he said, "Gina, everything your mother said is true. Every word. I love you, too. You are an exquisite ballerina."

"It's not true, Uncle Gene. I'll never be good enough!" Gina began to cry again. Gene stayed with her until she fell asleep.

Lily wrung her hands in frustration. This evening she was perched on Gina's dresser. "I was trying to help! Not make things worse!"

Chapter Twenty-Six

Gina and Gene were eating lunch. The dining room was Gina's favorite room, next to her bedroom. The maroon wallpaper and dark wooden rail that ran around the walls made her feel cozy and warm. In the past week Gina recovered from her recital. She had been working hard, practicing and listening to Ilya Alexandrovich. She tried to do all that he taught her. Gene insisted that she take time out for lunch with him.

The two were munching on sandwiches. Gina had taught Valerya Isidorovna how to put fillings in between two pieces of bread. For some reason she thought it was silly to make sandwiches, but Gene and Gina loved them.

"Gina you have been rehearsing a great deal for the White Nights Festival. Perhaps you need some rest from ballet. I suggest we host a Fourth of July party."

"Hey, Uncle Gene that's a great idea! Who should we have come?"

Gene shook his head. "You mean, who should we invite."

"Oh, stop. School's out." Gina smiled through a frown.

"That is no excuse for inelegant grammar," he said dodging an olive lobbed at his head by Gina. "And you learned that from your mother."

Gina giggled. "All right, who should we invite?"

"Tina, Nick, Ilya Alexandrovich, Tatiana Ivanovna, Tim, Lena and the baby, Harry, Valerya Isidorovna," Gene replied.

Gina sat down to make a list. "Do you think they'll do it, play baseball and eat American food and everything?"

"Sure, why not? And Miss Playwright-Ballerina, how about a costume or two?" Gene asked.

"That might be tough...I'll see what I can do. We have that baseball cap of yours. I'm sure Harry must have one around somewhere. I'll make hats out of red, white, and blue paper, too. We can buy huge, white t-shirts and write team names on them. People can put them on over their regular clothes. New York

Yankees and Minnesota Twins should be okay. What should we have to eat?" Gina continued writing her list.

"We brought popcorn from home, did we not?"

"Uncle Gene, that's perfect! We can wrap sausages in bread for hot dogs. Valerya Isidorovna has tons of pickles in the kitchen. We can buy ice-cream from the ice-cream man on the street. I'm sure Valerya Isidorovna will take me to the market to get lemons for lemonade, and watermelon. I bet she'd even bake a cake if we asked her!" Gina looked up. She dotted the last item on her list.

Gene looked at the list. "We must have American music. Perhaps we might sing *The Star-Spangled Banner* before I throw out the first ball? You may play some tapes of that pop music you brought with you."

"If you let me play my music, I guess I'll sing *The Star-Spangled Banner*. And since you're being so nice, we should play your Aaron Copeland tape. *Fanfare for the Common Man* and *Billy the Kid* would be fun." Gina added music to the list.

"And, what about fireworks? We can't have the Fourth of July without fireworks!"

"I shall procure sparklers for the occasion, Gina. Beware, though, Russians burn them inside the house. We shall have to insist that they be used only in the courtyard."

"Gosh, yes!" Gina exclaimed. "They burn sparklers inside their apartments? Well, I guess in a country where children drink tea, mail is delivered on Sundays, and the post office is open until eight o'clock at night, that's probably normal. I don't know why anything about Russia surprises me anymore."

All of the guests arrived at one in the afternoon on the dot on the Fourth of July. Very American behavior, right off the bat. Gina had never known any of her Russian friends to be on time for anything. This was a first. It was a sunny day, birds were singing. The guests stood around uncomfortably in the courtyard. At last they realized that the party was not going to be held in the apartment.

Gene and Gina had carried chairs down to the courtyard. They set up small tables that held the food, paper hats, and t-shirts. The guests noticed the tables with picnic food. They stood uncertainly by them. They were too polite to take a bite of a pickle or a drink of lemonade. Harry arrived. He generously helped himself to a hotdog moments after he arrived.

"Come on everybody! Dig in! You don't have to wait to be served at a Fourth of July party! These hotdogs are fantastic!" The Russian guests laughed and followed Harry's lead.

Gina whispered to Gene. "Uncle Gene, why don't our friends know how to act at this party?"

"The city of Leningrad is a city of apartments. There are no front or back lawns on which to play. The parks have walking paths. People are forbidden to walk on the grass in the parks," he explained.

Gina nodded. "Oh, yeah. I forgot about that. Even little kids stay by the park benches to play."

After everyone had eaten Gene announced, "Everyone, we are going to play baseball in the courtyard." The guests continued to stand hesitatingly.

"Everybody, put on a t-shirt with a team name and a hat!" Gina put on a t-shirt over her clothes and a paper hat to demonstrate.

Tina and Nick were chosen to play on the side of the Minnesota Twins along with Harry and Gina. Tim, Lena, Ilya Alexandrovich, and Gene played on the New York Yankees team. Ilya Alexandrovich even donned a red, white, and blue paper hat, which was a great joy to Gina. Valerya Isidorovna, Tatiana Ivanovna, and the baby, Misha, watched the game safely from their chairs.

"Gene, these are ping-pong paddles!" Gina hissed at her uncle. He picked up a ping-pong paddle and began to explain the rules of the game.

"It was all they had at the consulate. I just made the bases close together," he hissed back.

Gene explained the rules of American baseball. He acted things out furiously as he went along. Then he handed out the words to the national anthem. He made everyone sing along. He called out, "Play ball!" Then he threw out the first ball. He had always wanted to do that.

Gina whispered to Gene, "Isn't making them sing the English words of *The Star-Spangled Banner* sort of cheating? I mean, some of them didn't even know what they were singing."

"Oh, chill, Gina. For heaven's sake, it's a party!"

Gina smiled. It was as if Lily had taken over her uncle's personality. That was just what Lily would have said.

The highlight of the game was when Nick hit a sacrifice pop fly to get his cousin home. He had calculated her height, the length of her ballerina legs, and her known speed correctly. Gene fumbled the ball in the infield. Tina made a smashing grande jete' over home base as she ran in from third. Nick waved his arms wildly and shouted at her. She ran back and touched the home base that she had missed in her elegant flight over it.

Gina and Nick jumped up and down shouting, "We won! We won!"

Nick looked at Gina. "Gina, you are wonderful friend to have such magnificent party!" She felt Nick's arms tighten around her in a hug as he jumped up and down with her.

Lily almost fell off of her tree branch when she saw Nick hugging her daughter. Then she smiled. Lily liked Nick. He was good for Gina.

Chapter Twenty-Seven

Gene and Gina were at the consulate. Gene was getting a few last minute things together in his office. They were going together to Moscow, the capital city of Russia. Gene knew that Gina needed a break from her rehearsals. He decided to give Valerya Isidorovna a couple of days off and take Gina with him to Moscow.

"Uncle Gene, why are we going to Moscow?" Gina spun around in his leather desk chair.

Gene placed a file into his briefcase. "The American movie star, Jane Fonda, is in Moscow. She is going to jog around the Kremlin."

Gina continued spinning. "Why? And what's the Kremlin?"

Harry looked up from a sofa where he was reading the sports section of the newspaper. "She's advertising athletic shoes."

Gene laughed as he read from a press release. "Not exactly. Jane Fonda says she's promoting, 'good Russia – U.S. relations, and physical fitness.' The Kremlin is the center of power in Russia, like the capital in Washington, D.C. is in the United States."

"How unbelievably stupid," Harry said. "In a country wrestling with poverty and starvation, an American actress comes over to run around the Kremlin in crumbling Russia." He took the press release from Gene and read, "She is here, 'to bring the women of Russia running, walking, and physical exercise, with love, from the women of America.'" Gene put his head in his hands, "This could be worse than I thought."

Gina grabbed onto Gene's desk to stop spinning. "Harry, Uncle Gene, this is dumb. Doesn't she understand what is happening here? Doesn't she know how serious the situation is?"

Gene added two of his favorite pens to the briefcase. "Apparently not. So, Harry, how did you get out of this trip?"

Harry settled back onto the sofa and turned a page of the newspaper. "No one else wants to cover it. Even in Moscow. They're too busy with important matters. You're the Rookie, so you have to go. You'll get to meet Gorbachev."

"I will?" Gene tried to not show how excited he was at the prospect of meeting the president of Russia.

"Yeah, there's a press conference with Gorbachev and Fonda. We've already all met him. He's a good guy. I'll do all of your regular stuff, Gene. You need a break. Make a nice trip out of it." Harry was now fully stretched out on the sofa ready for a nap.

Gina was excited. "I don't know who Jane Fonda is, but I've never seen a movie star in person. And I've never even dreamed of meeting a president! Of any country!"

Tim dropped them at the train station. They rode the Krasnaya Strela, the Red Arrow train, that connected Leningrad and Moscow. They traveled at night in a coupe.' The compartment had beds that folded down out of the wall. Women who worked on the train brought Gina and Gene linens for their beds. Later they brought tea in podstakani with sugar. The following morning they brought tea and pastries as they pulled into the Moscow station.

Naturally, Lily decided to tag along. "This is so lovely. I've always wanted to ride on a train overnight!" She tucked herself into a corner of the compartment and rested.

Gene and Gina took a bus tour. They saw the shining golden domes of the Kremlin churches. They saw the wall of the Kremlin that surrounded the city and Red Square. They went inside the colorful St. Basil's Cathedral. It looked more like a palace from Disneyland than a church.

They went to the Armory. The Armory held crown jewels from the days of the tsars and tsaritsas, the kings and queens. There were vases and trays made of silver, gold, and gems from kings and queens of other countries. There were the beautiful eggs designed by Faberge'. There were rooms filled with golden Cinderella coaches and gem-encrusted costumes for coronations. Gina saw a room filled with tiny costumes. "Are those for kids?"

He replied, "No, Gina. Those were the clothes of the court dwarves."

Gina stared at a tiny silk overcoat and pants. "Wait. What? Dwarves?"

Gene pointed to a tiny ball gown. "Yes. They were kept as companions for the tsars and tsaritsas. They acted mainly as clowns, to entertain."

"That is so weird, Uncle Gene."

Gina followed Gene onto the next display of costumes. "I suppose it was. Although at the time life was difficult. People were poor. To serve for the tsar was an honor."

Later that afternoon, Gina and Gene were admitted to an office in the Kremlin. Members of the press, Gene, and Gina were invited to tea with President Gorbachev and Jane Fonda. They entered a large room and sat at a table reserved for reporters.

"Uncle Gene, he's so little," Gina said in surprise.

"He is, that." Gene smiled.

Jane Fonda made a speech about aerobic physical fitness. She stressed the importance of Russians pursuing healthier habits.

Lily rolled her eyes as she shimmered, hanging onto a chandelier. "Gene was right. This is silly for an actress to be blaming people about their health when things are so difficult."

President Gorbachev agreed with Jane's comments about physical fitness, through an interpreter. President Gorbachev rose. He expressed a desire to meet the members of the press. The correspondents formed a line.

President Gorbachev greeted and shook the hand of each person. Gene waved away an interpreter when his turn came. In perfect Russian he congratulated the President on his work in moving Russia toward democracy. Mikhail Gorbachev looked gratefully into Gene's eyes and warmly embraced him. He kissed Gene's cheeks three times as Russian men do.

Gina smiled. She said "Hello" in Russian as her uncle had taught her, "Zdrastvooitye, Mikhail Sergeyevich." Behind the smiles and handshakes, eight KGB agents did not leave President Gorbachev's side for an instant. The KGB protected President Gorbachev the same way the Secret Service protected President Bush.

Lily jumped the line. She took President Gorbachev's hand as he offered it to a journalist from Australia. President Gorbachev remarked upon the coldness of the man's hand. Both men were confused. The journalist had a notebook in one hand and a pen in the other. The President remarked that the day had been long and he was somewhat tired. He shook the journalist's hand. Lily smiled and softly skipped away.

After the conference, Gene remarked, "He is a great man, Gina. There is no doubt. He is slowly trying to give small countries like Estonia and Lithuania their own power."

Gina stopped at a refreshment table and took a cookie. "Uncle Gene, I still don't understand. What does that mean?"

Gene crunched on a cookie. "President Gorbachev giving the small countries their own power? It is similar to a situation in American history. If Britain had freely given the U.S. our power when we broke away from England over two hundred years ago, that would have been like what he is trying to do. Instead we had the revolutionary war with Britain to gain our independence."

"If the people are so mad and they don't want to wait, why don't Estonia and Lithuania have a revolutionary war?" Gina sipped a cherry compote.

"They are poor and small countries. President Gorbachev has given them hope that they can have their own power," explained Gene.

"Which countries want to be free?" Gina asked.

Gene led her slowly through the crowd of journalists. "I know for certain that Estonia, Lithuania, and Latvia are already working toward their independence. Probably the Ukraine and Kazakhstan are as well."

Gina hung on to her uncle's elbow. "Okay, tell me more. I'm trying to understand."

Gene held the door for several older journalists and Gina. "President Gorbachev wrote a Union Treaty. The treaty strengthens the powers of the small countries. The treaty would give the small countries more control over their finances and natural resources. President Gorbachev is facing stiff resistance to the treaty from the Russian men who are in power over the small countries. They do not want to give their power away."

"But, won't it be better for everyone if the small countries each have their own power?" Gina asked as they made it to the outer door and stepped out onto the street.

"Yes. President Gorbachev continues to struggle to drag Russia into the modern age," Gene commented. "In history he will be remembered as a great leader."

The two had dinner at a Turkish restaurant near their hotel. Gene loved the restaurant. He had dined there many years ago. It had not changed. On the first floor of the restaurant there were open bins of spices, coffees, and teas for sale. The warm, spicy smells were wonderful. The restaurant was in a loft on the second floor. Gene and Gina climbed the wooden stairs to the low tables and couches where they had dinner.

They had lamb, rice, and salads with olives. Gene had coffee at the end. Gina watched the waiter put coffee and water into a metal cup with a wooden handle. This he placed in a box of very hot sand. There the metal cup sat until it bubbled over. The coffee was poured into a tiny cup to be drunk with sugar.

Then they went to the station. They rode the Krasnaya Strela night train back to Leningrad. After tea and breakfast they arrived at the station, ready to begin the day.

Chapter Twenty-Eight

The girls were on their way to the United States Consulate to visit Gina's uncle. They walked slowly along the quiet shady street eating cranberries dipped in powdered sugar.

"I never dreamed I could visit U.S. consulate, Gina! No Russian citizens are allowed to enter without very special permission." Tina threw a cranberry into the air and caught it in her mouth.

"Well, I could never have gotten into the Kirov Academy without you and your father, Tina!"

"Consulate is pink!" Tina stood and stared as they neared the building.

Gina stood next to her. "Yeah, I know. I thought it would be red, white and blue."

They entered through the heavy, wooden outer door. Gina showed her United States passport to the guard on duty. He sat on an elevated chair that was behind glass and iron bars. Tina showed her Russian passport and both girls were allowed to enter. Tina was only permitted to go into the consulate because she was the guest of a U.S. citizen.

The second guard in the lobby was new. He did not know Gina. He checked the girls' passports again. "Go home to the U.S. Things are very bad in Leningrad. Where are your parents?"

Gina accepted the passport he handed back to her. "I'm here with my uncle, Dr. Shostek."

"Gene? Well, he should have enough sense to send you home! The government is ready to crash any minute!" He waved them into the newsroom.

The girls went into the large, round newsroom. They glanced at what news coming over the wire. Usually consulate employees were smiling and welcoming. Today they angrily stomped back and forth across the room to offices that surrounded the newsroom.

A door opened. Gina caught a glimpse of her uncle in a meeting with Harry. Gene looked angry and about to explode. The girls overheard Harry telling Gene to stop writing the daily report. "Gene, quit sending the stuff every day to D.C.! They're not reading the local news anymore. They're looking for the big stuff. President Gorbachev or Prime Minister Ligachev! Give yourself a break!"

Gene growled back to Harry, "It is my job. I do not know what else to do!" The girls thought it best to leave.

Out on the street Gina asked, "Tina what do you know about what's going on?"

"It is complex. People have no food and no money. They want President Gorbachev out. They want democracy, but they want it fast. They do not want to wait for his plans. They say he is too slow. Little Estonia, Latvia, Kazakhstan, and all others want to be own countries. President Gorbachev is letting them go step by step, but they want it quick!"

The girls bought more cranberries. The little stand on the street was the only place you could buy them in Leningrad. "Tina, Why isn't there any food or money?"

"Because much food is grown in southern countries. They do not want to transport and sell products to Russia unless they are let go from Russia's control."

Tina continued, "There is no money because no one wants to buy or sell anything until they know what banks will protect money. Will it be new Russian bank or new bank? Who knows? Gina, I cannot explain all to you. I do not understand all. I only know what papa tells me."

Gina saw how her friend worried. "Me, too, I guess. I saw bigger crowds by the Kazan Cathedral when I walked with my uncle. He said they talk about politics there out in the open."

Tina walked along beside Gina. "Yes, people no longer fear jail for talking against government. For many years people only talked in homes with curtains shut so government could not know what was said."

"There is food at home and at the consulate. Why is that?" Gina asked innocently.

"Because you are foreigner, food is flown here for you on airplane from Finland. Finland is free country like United States," Tina explained.

Gina wondered, "Tina, how can I help?"

Tina smiled at her friend. "You cannot. Maybe someday you write story about us. Beautiful, sad story about old Russia. How Russia is like forest in your mother's story. It is chaos and no one can put it to rights!"

The girls parted under the arches on Rubenstein Street. They went to their apartments. Gina went to her spacious apartment that had been provided by the United States consulate. Tina went to her small apartment that had been willed to Ilya Alexandrovich by Tina's grandfather. No one in the city of Leningrad lived in private homes, as Gina would when she returned to the U.S.

Gina was relieved Gene was still at work. She would have some time alone in the apartment. Gina could hardly stand being in the apartment with Gene anymore. He was always tense and distracted. Gina thought he was irritable. He kept losing things, his keys, his notebooks, his maps. Once she saw him snap at Tim and then apologize.

Gina was still preparing for the White Nights Festival performance with Ilya Alexandrovich. She was feeling pretty tense herself. She practiced in her room, in the study, and in the dining room. She even practiced in the kitchen, until Valerya Isidorovna shooed her away. She knew all of the steps by heart. She did everything Ilya Alexandrovich told her to do.

Dancing didn't feel any more emotional, passionate or special than it ever had. She was less afraid, but that was all. "I'm never going to find courage or have passion or anything!" she thought after practicing. "I blew it at my recital from the academy. That was with students at my own level. Now I have to dance a solo! I can't do this! What was Ilya Alexandrovich thinking!?"

Days went by. Gina's mood did not improve. She quarreled with Valerya Isidorovna over some little thing that didn't matter. She even quarreled with Tina. Tina had come by to see Gina. Tina watched her dance the piece she was preparing for the White Nights Festival. Gina wanted to have an audience before she had to dance on stage alone in front of lots of people.

"Gina, it is beautiful. Papa will like. I told Nick to come to White Nights Festival to see you dance. He said he will come. You know he likes you. I told him you like him, too!" Tina said after Gina finished dancing.

Gina was shocked. "You told Nick that I like him?!" How could you?"

"I want only to help. You were sad about Max." Tina's face showed that she was afraid that she had hurt Gina.

"I don't even know myself if I like Nick! I can't believe you told him! That is so unfair!" Gina said angrily.

"Gina, please be calm. I am sorry. I will go now," Tina said. She left the room and then the apartment. Gina did not try to stop her or go after her.

Gina went back to her room and sat on the edge of her bed. She detested everyone and everything, but especially herself. "Why can't I be like Tina? Why can't I be beautiful, talented, and giving like her? Or, why can't I be like Valerya Isidorovna and not want to be an artist at all. Why can't I be happy going to school and becoming a boring, old lawyer, or something like that?"

Lily flitted nervously across the ceiling. She whispered, "Gina, I wish I could help you with this. I have to let you get through these feelings yourself. Besides, right now you wouldn't listen to me anyway!"

Gina interrupted her uncle that night. He was putting on his cap and preparing to go out and get details of the changing political scene. Gina crossed her arms over her chest and leaned on the doorframe of his bedroom. "Uncle Gene, I don't think you should go tonight. I have a bad feeling. The sun never setting makes people crazy."

Gene said tensely. "True, it is a scientific fact that we are located at a longitude so near the North Pole that for several weeks surrounding the summer solstice, the sun sets for only a few hours each night. There is no evidence to support a relation between the lack of sunset and the mental health of the people in St. Petersburg!"

"It's still called Leningrad, Uncle Gene."

Gene did not look at her as he said. "Not for much longer. Return to bed. I will be in after you have fallen asleep. Valerya Isidorovna is here to stay with you. Now, go!"

Gina crawled into bed, but sat straight up with her eyes wide open. She was worried. At two in the morning she heard a car pull up outside. She looked out onto the bright courtyard below. Harry was helping Gene through the doorway. In the sunlight Gina saw blood on his face. Gina raced out to the kitchen as the two men entered. "Gina, do not become excited. It was a minor skirmish. I am quite fine."

Gina rushed to get a towel and dabbed at her uncle's face. "You're not fine! Wow, what a shiner! What happened?"

Getting ice from the freezer, Harry said, "For some reason your uncle thought it would be a swell idea to listen to the political discussions at the Kazan, even though every last one of us at the consulate was warned to stay away. Two men were murdered there last week. People are crazy! No one knows what's going to happen! All they know is that something is going to happen!"

Gina continued to dab, trying hard not to look at the bloody towel. "But why were they mad at you? You're trying to help."

Gene sat down. Harry placed an icepack on his aching head. "Two men figured out from my accent that I am an American. Russians are hungry, angry, and have no hope for the future. They believe that all Americans are rich and happy as they see in the movies. Their jealousy incited them to anger and then to violence. I luckily slipped out of their grasp. I ran to Harry's apartment without them following me."

Gina ran cold water over the towel. "Uncle Gene, maybe you should stop doing that report to Washington, D.C. every day. "

"Listen to your niece, Gene. I've told you." Harry pleaded. The ice pack had slipped and Gina had applied a fresh towel.

Gene had some trouble speaking through them. His shouted voice was muffled. "Absolutely not! I will not be intimidated by a couple of hotheads. I must continue to try to find out exactly what is happening with this country! I will complete my assignment to the best of my ability."

"Might be tough to do that assignment if you wind up in the hospital, or dead in some alley," Harry said, looking Gene in the eye as he opened the door to leave.

No one slept much that night, in Gene and Gina's apartment, or in all of Russia.

Chapter Twenty-Nine

"President Gorbachev is missing! No one is running the country!" Harry huffed and puffed as he ended his run to the consulate, rushing past Gina, and bursting into Gene's office. "Gene, for heaven's sake, Palace Square is filling up. Didn't you hear the radio?" Gene looked up from his daily report.

Gina was waiting in the newsroom for her uncle. In a few minutes they would leave to go to her performance for the White Nights Festival. She nervously shifted from one foot to the other. She wanted to get to the theater early to have time to warm up before her solo.

Gene turned up the volume on the radio and listened. In horror he heard classical music and nothing else. No commentary, no voices, nothing. Only the strains of *Swan Lake* played over and over. In Russia when there is a major political problem, all broadcasts are stopped until the government decides what they want the people to know. Everyone in Russia knew that a radio transmitting only classical music meant that the country was at war, or that something terrible had happened.

Gene ran to the teletype in the newsroom. He read the report that had been lying on the machine since he came in that morning. "President Mikhail Gorbachev can no longer perform his duties due to ill health, the official news agency TASS reported Sunday night, August 18, 1991. The location of President Gorbachev is not known. A fatal danger is hanging over Russia. All Russian radio stations are playing classical music, as they have in the past when there has been a change in president."

Gene clenched his teeth. He mentally kicked himself for not checking the wire when he arrived at the office. The teletype came to life and started printing loudly. "President Gorbachev was to have flown to Moscow on Tuesday, August 20, to sign the new Union Treaty giving more powers to small countries under Russian rule."

Reports continued to pour in. "General Moiseyev, a military chief, claims to be the new president of Russia. Moiseyev has taken power from President Gorbachev, saying the president is in ill health. Hundreds of tanks and other military vehicles have moved into Moscow to assist Moiseyev in his climb to power."

Gene looked up from the report in his hands in disbelief. "Harry, this is craziness. Russia has fallen apart! Where is Gorbachev?"

More printed. "Palace Square in St. Petersburg, formerly known as Leningrad, is filling with thousands of citizens waiting for news of Gorbachev."

"Uncle Gene, I have to go! I'll be late!" Gina cried from the lobby. She bounded out the door.

Gene slammed his fist on his desk when he realized Gina was gone. Gina's performance was going to begin in an hour at the Kirov Theater. Gina would have to go through Palace Square and the thousands of people gathering there to get to the Kirov. Gene shouted to Harry who was stuffing film into a 35mm camera, "I am leaving for Palace Square!"

Harry looked up and hurried after him. "Not without me, you're not!"

Gina made it to Palace Square. She did not understand why Palace Square was filling with people. She understood some of the words she heard. She could not understand enough to know the reason for thousands of people to gather in the small square near the Winter Palace. Tina could have helped her figure out what was happening. Since they had quarreled, Gina had not called Tina to go to the performance together.

Gina knew she must go to perform at the White Nights Festival, but she dreaded dancing. Her final rehearsal had not gone well. She could not make herself call Tina for advice. Ilya Alexandrovich was the director and had to think of all of the dancers. He had no time for Gina's frustrations. She imagined Tina was still mad at her. Gina didn't blame her.

She held her dance bag close to protect herself from the crowd. She made her way out of the square and onto a side street that led to the theater. She remembered her mother telling her that emotional times are the best times to dance. Gina knew that she could pretend to be lost in the crowd. She could make excuses later that she couldn't make it to the performance because of the crowds. She was going to the theater because she was Gina. And she went because she was an artist, almost a professional ballerina, Gina thought with pride.

She started to run and entered the backstage area puffing. Hardly anyone was there. Five or six musicians out of the whole orchestra, a handful of audience members, and Ilya Alexandrovich. A few other dancers. The conductor had not made it to the theater. Ilya Alexandrovich would conduct the orchestra. Ilya Alexandrovich quickly told the musicians changes in the arrangements to cover for missing musicians. Everyone made notes in their music.

Ilya Alexandrovich tapped a baton on the music stand. He announced to the tiny audience that the concert would be played full length, although with many instruments missing. He asked the small audience, the musicians, and dancers to pray for hope for their country, for the safe return of President Gorbachev, and for peace and prosperity.

Gina quickly went to the dressing room to get into make-up and costume. Gina understood the notes and where silences would come in the music because musicians were missing. Her Russian was not good enough to understand the last part about President Gorbachev. Gina worried about Gene. Where was he? What if he was in Palace Square looking for her? What if he came across those men that had beaten him up?

Gina breathed lightly and finished tying her pointe shoe ribbons. She took her place backstage and warmed up. There was no ballet mistress there to lead the dancers through a class. In the wings, she held on to the back of a chair to practice grande plie's and tendus.

She suddenly felt a wave of nausea. Gina was horrified. Her first solo, and she was more terrified than she had ever been about dancing on stage! She breathed slowly and smiled. She smelled her mother's *Joy* perfume.

Lily placed a cool hand on her daughter's warm forehead. Then Lily kissed Gina lightly on the cheek.

Gina smiled again and relaxed. She waited in the wings until the dancers before her finished their piece. She heard applause. The lights went down. She took her place on stage. She stepped out onto the wooden floor and found her mark at center stage. The lights went up. She looked into Ilya Alexandrovich's eyes. He gave her a warm smile and signaled the musicians to begin. She followed Ilya Alexandrovich's baton out of the corner of her eye.

She danced through the silent parts. She floated through the difficult choreography. She gently and powerfully executed each step. With each step she told the story of her mother becoming sick, and then dying. She told the story of missing Lily, and knowing that her mom was in heaven.

The music faded and Gina bowed to the few people in the audience. They clapped loudly and long.

Lily clapped the longest and most enthusiastically, although no one could hear her.

Gina knew that she had danced with emotion and brilliantly. "I found my courage," she thought. Gina felt like she was worth all of the diamonds and rubies and jewels in the world. Gina watched the other dancers perform. She went to the dressing room and changed back into street clothes.

Music and ballet were her friends now. She knew they would never leave her. She loved ballet so much, Gina thought. Now dance was tangled up with her love for her mom, Uncle Gene, and Ilya Alexandrovich. It was entwined with her friendships with Tina and Nick.

Dance was part of the air and the theater and everyone around her. It was part of all of those people out there in Palace Square. Gina felt that what had happened to her was as large as whatever it was that was happening in Russia.

After the concert was over Ilya Alexandrovich put his hand on her shoulder. Everyone else had gone back into the streets to find out the latest news. "My dear, now you are one of us. You shall grow old with pointe shoes, I think."

"And I'm going to have lots of great stories to tell with them!" Gina said as she stuffed her pointe shoes into her bag. "You will my dear. Now we must go to Palace Square and find Tina and Nick. I think your uncle must be there as well." He started toward the door of the theater with Gina following.

Gina flung the big dance bag over her shoulder. "Do you think they are there?"

"When you were late Tina and Nick insisted going to find you. I cautioned against it." Ilya Alexandrovich opened the heavy outer door for them.

Gina took her bag off of her shoulder and threw it into Ilya Alexandrovich's arms. As he caught the bag she ran past him out into the street. "Then you have to stay here in case they come back or they won't know where you are!" Gina cried.

Ilya Alexandrovich fell back slightly from the weight of the dance bag. He tried to follow. He soon lost sight of Gina in the crowded streets.

Chapter Thirty

Gina saw from a distance that Palace Square was terrifyingly full of pressing crowds. The crowds were waiting for officials to come out of the Senate Building, across from the Hermitage Museum and the Winter Palace, to give news of President Gorbachev.

Gina saw the tall Alexandrine Monument in the middle of the square. Most of the people had gathered around it. Gina thought of the Space Needle at the State Fair. She headed for the Alexandrine Monument.

"Hope Uncle Gene remembers what I'm remembering," she fleetingly thought. She snaked her way through the crowd.

Lily floated in the air above Gina, "Meet at the Space Needle if you get lost" she thought. Gina had figured it out. That left only Gene. Lily chuckled when she saw Gene. He was fighting with Harry to go into the thick of the crowd to find his niece. Harry insisted that Gina was safe and sound either at home, or at the concert hall with Ilya Alexandrovich. Gene ripped his arm away from Harry and dove into the crowds. Harry followed him. "I didn't know he had it in him!" Lily laughed. Lily darted over to Gene. She whispered, "Space Needle," into his ear.

Gene grabbed Harry. "I know where she is!" Harry and Gene found Gina waiting by the Alexandrine Monument. It did look like the Space Needle! Gina screamed and waved her arms until they could make their way to her. Gene embraced his niece gratefully.

The three, being in the center, had the best vantage point to see and hear the people speaking. Harry snapped pictures madly. Gene listened and translated. Gina wrote it all down. After an hour or so they raced back to the consulate. Gene and Harry turned in the first report to Washington, D.C. of this important event.

The three sat down to rest. They were delighted when the words they had moments ago faxed to Washington, D.C. came back to them in an official news report over the teletype.

"It was reported today from Palace Square, that President Mikhail Gorbachev had been at the airport about to board the presidential plane to fly Moscow to sign the Union Treaty. President Gorbachev was arrested, forced into a helicopter, and flown to an airbase in southern Russia. During the coup, President Gorbachev refused to resign as president of Russia. President Gorbachev was removed from his position against his will, and was held by force. He was not in ill health, as was previously reported."

Gina immediately telephoned Tina at home. She was relieved that the phone worked and that Tatiana Ivanovna answered.

"Tatiana Ivanovna, are you okay? Is everyone else okay? My uncle and Harry and I are here at the consulate!" Gina asked breathlessly.

"Yes, we are fine. Tina and Ilya are here. Nick is here with us. Tina will go to tell Valerya Isidorovna that you are at consulate and will give food to Sugarplum." Then the phone crackled and went dead.

Gina hung up. She was happy that the Mikhailovs had reached their apartment safely. Gene, Gina and Harry stayed all night at the consulate for protection and to read the news.

"It was reported from Palace Square, that on Wednesday, August 21, 1991, the national legislature has demanded that President Gorbachev be president. President Gorbachev has headed to Moscow to assume power again. The Union Treaty that gives powers to small countries such as Latvia, Lithuania, and Kazakhstan, is in effect. "

"Why's it called a coup?" Gina asked her uncle. They were finally allowed to leave the consulate and be driven to their apartment by Tim.

"It's from the French. It is accurately called coup d'etat. A coup d'etat is the taking of government power by a small group. This coup d'etat was not successful. The most powerful men in government could not be shaken. They want President Gorbachev to return to lead them."

"Uncle Gene, I'm tired. And I'm scared. Can I go stay with Tina tonight? Or can she come here? If she'll talk to me again, anyway."

"I think Tina spending the night here is an excellent idea. And no late night!" Gene warned.

Gina looked over at him. "And no going out tonight for you either!"

"No problem there, dear Gina." Gene sheepishly smiled. He still had a bit of a black eye.

Gina called Tina. Before the telephone stopped ringing in the Mikhailov apartment, Tina appeared, banging on the Shosteks' door. "Gina, I knew it was you! I have come to spend night." They turned and waved "Good-bye" to Nick who had escorted Tina through the courtyard.

"You're not mad at me? Gina asked. She threw her arms around Tina. Tina, surprised and pleased at Gina's show of emotion, answered, "No, dear. I saw whole performance at White Nights Festival. Nick and I watched like mice in back of theater. You are genius!"

They leaned out the window to hear Nick call, "Gina, you are most beautiful ballerina in all world!" Gina accepted her friends' compliments. She hugged Tina again.

"But I can't figure out why I wasn't scared." Gina remarked. "I had so much fun dancing. I didn't think about making mistakes at all! I felt like I was in heaven!"

"What was different from other times you have danced?" asked Tina. "Was it because you were in new theater? Because audience was not so large?"

"Tina, I know this sounds dumb, but I smelled my mom's perfume right before I went on. This is even weirder. I felt her hand on my forehead. I felt her kiss me on the cheek! It was so nice when Ilya Alexandrovich smiled at me before I started dancing."

"That is not weird! That is how I feel when papa watches me. I also have little trick for when he is not in audience," said Tina.

"Well, tell me! What is it?" Gina asked. She grabbed Tina's shoulders.

Tina laughed. "It is simple. I sew small, blue forget-me-not flower into costume where no one can see. It reminds me that papa will not forget me. Many performers do such things. Papa wears watch on wrong wrist when he is choreographing. He says it makes ideas come faster. Max puts kopeck in shoe whenever he has solo. He says it makes him play best."

"What should I do? No, wait, I've got it! I have a lace handkerchief of my mom's with Lily embroidered on it. I can put some of her perfume on it. I can tuck it into the bodice of my costume whenever I perform! I can't wait to try it out!" Gina exclaimed.

"Listen to you! Not wanting to wait until next performance! I knew this would happen for you," said Tina. She hugged her friend.

Chapter Thirty-One

The girls waited in the apartment the next day until Gene returned from the consulate. Gene informed the two that although President Gorbachev was again in power, the country was in chaos. Word had arrived from Washington, D.C. "All nonessentials at the consulate must return to the United States."

"I don't know if I want to be something called a nonessential," Gina joked.

"It is a term. It means that the consulate can operate without us. In any event, it is time to pack our belongings and return home. We are to leave tomorrow," Gene said. Tina and Valerya Isidorovna sat with them around the dining room table. "Tomorrow! But that doesn't even give us time to say good-bye!" Gina declared.

"We shall simply have to make do. Mama, papa, and Nick shall come and help to pack," Tina offered. She picked up the telephone to call her family.

Valerya Isidorovna went into the kitchen to prepare a farewell dinner. Dinner was somber and joyful at the same time. Tim, Lena, and the baby came for dinner, too. Gene called Harry to come also. Many photos were taken.

Nick brought flowers for Gina. She shyly accepted them. She gave the bouquet a place of honor in the center of the dining room table. Everyone tried not to notice too much that Gina invited Nick to sit next to her at dinner. Tina sat on her other side.

The Russians, fond of toasting, raised many glasses to Gene and Gina. Harry told them that he would remain in St. Petersburg. He was essential to the operations of the consulate. Tim would become Harry's chauffeur. All of the dinner guests, Gene, and Gina set to work to pack up all they could that evening. Harry assured them that he would send the rest.

After dinner Gina returned Sugarplum to Tina. "Tina, thank you for letting me take care of Sugarplum. I love her! Good luck with examinations every year at the academy. I know you won't need it!"

"Ballerinas always need luck. Thank you, Gina. When government settles down come to visit!"

"After graduation, we dance together all over the world!" they shouted.

Saying "Good-bye" to Tina's uncle was easier. She would see Ilya Alexandrovich when he toured with the Kirov ballet company in the United States.

"Ilya Alexandrovich, thank you for everything you have done for me! I am so grateful to you and Tina for helping me learn to dance."

Ilya Alexandrovich smiled. "Gina, it is my work. Keep pointing toes."

Everyone thoughtfully left so Gina could say "Good-bye" to Nick alone.

"Gina, we shall write letters, yes? I will tell all about new inventions. When we see each other again you will know all about me!" He put his arms around her and hugged her.

Gina returned his hug. She said, "Yes, and maybe I'll even learn enough to write to you in Russian!"

Lily protectively watched from the ceiling corner of the foyer. She bashed her head on the light fixture when she saw Gina give Nick a kiss! "I thought she'd at least wait for him to kiss her. She's only twelve! And on the lips!"

Gina thought to herself, "I'm almost thirteen! Plenty old enough to kiss a boy!"

Just then Gene came down the hall to see her to bed. He shook Nick's hand. "I will miss you very much, Nick. You have a great future ahead of you. You are a brilliant young man."

"Thank you, sir. I will see you both at airport tomorrow. Good-bye!" The door shut behind him. Gina went to get ready for bed.

In the morning Gene was reflective. "I know that Russia has been changed forever. It will never be the place that I knew during the days of my studies at the university," Gene said to Gina.

He was packing their last few things in the living room. "I hope that conditions improve for the residents of St. Petersburg and everywhere else in the country. It's official. The city is no longer called Leningrad. It is St. Petersburg."

Gina carefully placed several pairs of new pointe shoes into her suitcase. They were a gift from Tina. "Uncle Gene, do you think Tina could visit sometime?"

Gene clicked one of his suitcases shut. "I arranged for an official invitation for Tina and Nick at the consulate. They can come and visit as our guests whenever they like. I issued invitations to both so Tina would not travel alone. I have one more surprise that I think you will like."

"They can visit? Uncle Gene, that is fantastic! What's the surprise?"

Gene sat on the sofa. "Gina, I have arranged to take a position at Columbia University. We are moving to New York City. Nijinsky will join us. I have also arranged for you to audition for the School of American Ballet in New York. Ilya Alexandrovich thinks it is the best place for you now."

"Wow! New York! Mom loved dancing there! Thank you, Uncle Gene! I'm so excited! I'm really going to become a ballerina!" Gina danced around the sofa and her uncle.

Gene grabbed a few more books to pack from the coffee table. "I am surprised you are not requesting that Tina be our permanent guest."

Gina took the books from him and packed them in another waiting suitcase. "Tina has to finish school here. She goes to the best ballet school in the world. We will go everywhere together when we're both done with school!"

They left the apartment and went down to meet Tim. They piled into the car with their luggage. Valerya Isidorovna waved "Good-bye" as they drove out of the courtyard. Gina watched as she turned away and went back into the apartment building. Gina was happy to be going home, but she would miss everyone so much. Thank heaven Nijinsky was waiting for her.

Lily swooped and flew along above the car. "Gina, I love you so. I wish I could be with you. Sometimes I think I'm helping you more now than ever. New York City will be lovely!"

Many people who loved Gina and Gene came to say "Good-bye." There was barely room at the airport for all of them. Nick stayed long after everyone left. He watched the plane taxi down the runway, gather speed, and lift off up into the clouds.

The End

Made in the USA
Charleston, SC
15 May 2015